Tyler was a very attractive man

With his dark hair and unusual silver-gray eyes, that bump in his nose and the decisive shape of his jaw and forehead, he was easily the best-looking man Ally had shared a meal with in a long time.

Then there was his body.

Broad, hard, lean, with the kind of muscles that came from doing things in the real world rather than pumping iron in the gym...

Ally felt a tightening low in her belly.

A slow grin curled his mouth. For a moment she forgot how and why they'd met, forgot that he was exactly the kind of man she usually avoided. It was a warm, balmy night and the world seemed ripe with possibilities.

It was only her, and him.

Dear Reader,

I have always been fascinated by advice columns. A really good one can keep me in its thrall for years, eagerly awaiting new editions of whichever magazine or newspaper it appears in. It's not so much the solutions that fascinate me—although I am a big fan of common sense!—but the problems that people are dealing with. Believe me, after years of being an assiduous (some might say obsessive) online reader of the Dear Prudence column at *Slate* magazine, truth is definitely stranger than fiction. Definitely.

Given my little obsession, it's probably not a huge surprise that it would make its way into my writing—my heroine in *The Last Goodbye*, Ally, is an advice columnist. Interested and bright and accepting, Ally does her best to respond to readers looking for compassion, a slap on the wrist or instruction on how to navigate the waters of wedding etiquette. The ironic thing is, Ally's own life is far from perfect. She's a born gypsy, traveling from place to place, living out of her suitcase. She's convinced she'll never settle down—that she can't, in fact—until she meets Tyler. As we all know, falling in love is the ultimate game changer.

I hope you enjoy this book. I love to hear from readers—you can contact me via my website at www.sarahmayberry.com.

Until next time,

Sarah Mayberry

The Last Goodbye
Sarah Mayberry

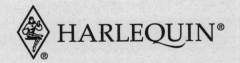

TORONTO • NEW YORK • LONDON
AMSTERDAM • PARIS • SYDNEY • HAMBURG
STOCKHOLM • ATHENS • TOKYO • MILAN • MADRID
PRAGUE • WARSAW • BUDAPEST • AUCKLAND

Recycling programs
for this product may
not exist in your area.

ISBN-13: 978-0-373-71686-9

THE LAST GOODBYE

www.eHarlequin.com

Printed in U.S.A.

ABOUT THE AUTHOR

Sarah Mayberry lives in Melbourne in a house that needs much renovating, and she's praying for the day when someone invents self-stripping wallpaper. When she's not writing romance novels or stripping wallpaper, she works as a freelance script writer and story consultant for the Australian and New Zealand TV industries. She loves reading, movies, cooking and sleeping. And not necessarily in that order...

Books by Sarah Mayberry

HARLEQUIN SUPERROMANCE

HARLEQUIN BLAZE

Don't miss any of our special offers. Write to us at the following address for information on our newest releases.

Harlequin Reader Service
U.S.: 3010 Walden Ave., P.O. Box 1325, Buffalo, NY 14269
Canadian: P.O. Box 609, Fort Erie, Ont. L2A 5X3

This one is definitely for Chris.
Thank you for holding my hand,
for workshopping scenes,
and for setting me straight on more than one
occasion. You are the best friend, mentor, partner,
lover and sidekick a woman could ever ask for.

Thanks also to Wanda, who trims my excesses
and reminds me of all the things I thought I'd
learned absolutely with the last book. Bless you!

I'd also like to acknowledge my father—
Dad, I love you very much.
Thank you from the bottom of my heart
for being one of the good ones.

CHAPTER ONE

TYLER ADAMSON SMOOTHED his hand over the surface of the newly sanded tabletop. The mahogany was warm and smooth as silk and by the time one of his team had rubbed several layers of shellac into it, the wood grain beneath his fingers would glow with a deep red luster. Amazing to think that mere weeks ago this finely honed piece of furniture had been nothing but a pile of roughly hewn wood and an idea on his drawing board.

"When is this scheduled for delivery?" he asked as he stepped back from the table.

His senior cabinetmaker, Dino, rolled his eyes. "Relax. It's on schedule. Go away and design something." He made a shooing motion with his hands.

Tyler ignored him, his gaze sweeping the crowded workshop. A Georgian sideboard was awaiting final sanding and a desk was in the process of having leather inlaid into its surface. A dozen balloon-back rosewood chairs were stacked to one side, ready to be upholstered, while no less than three dining tables were at various stages of assembly.

"Let Gabby know if you need another pair of hands," he said as he turned away.

He'd put too much time and effort into building the business to blow it by letting customers down with long delays now that business was booming.

"She'll hear about it, don't worry," Dino said.

Tyler didn't doubt it. Dino had never been shy about voicing his opinion in the past, after all. Tyler started toward the stairs to his mezzanine workspace, only to change direction when he remembered he'd left the notes from his recent client meeting in his truck. He passed the administration office, where he could see Gabby talking on the phone, then cut across the plush carpeted showroom to the front entrance.

The parking lot was baking in the late-afternoon sun, heat shimmering on the tarmac. He crossed to his truck, grabbed the folder off the rear seat, then headed for the coolness of the building.

"Tyler Adamson?"

He glanced over his shoulder to see a small, dark-haired woman bearing down on him.

"That's me. How can I help you?" he asked.

"My name's Ally Bishop."

She looked at him expectantly, clearly waiting for him to recognize her. He frowned. Her face was round, her eyes big and brown and her hair cut close to her head. She looked like she should be wearing an elf costume as part of Santa's Kingdom at the mall.

Definitely he'd never met her before.

"I'm sorry, but if this is about an order, you're better off speaking to Gabby. I'm a little out of the loop on where we're at with lead times right now."

He offered her a smile, inviting her to be amused by his administrative incompetence.

She crossed her arms over her chest and glared at him as though he'd clubbed a baby seal to death in front of a class of preschoolers.

"I called you yesterday. I'm the one who left the message about your father being in hospital," she said.

Tyler stilled. "What?"

"He didn't want me to call you. He said you didn't have time for him, but I thought you might find room in your busy schedule to visit. Clearly, I was wrong."

She was starting to get red in the face and he got the feeling she was only warming up.

He held up a hand. "Hold on a minute—my father's in hospital?"

"Didn't you get my message?" She sounded suspicious. As though she thought he was lying to make himself look better.

"We had some water damage here a few weeks ago when that big storm came through. The answering machine's been on the blink ever since."

"Right." She frowned. He could practically hear her trying to change gears as she reassessed her opinion of him.

"What's wrong with him?" he asked.

He wanted to take the words back as soon as they'd left his mouth. He'd decided long ago to draw a line under his relationship with his father. Him being sick didn't change that.

"He collapsed in the backyard with stomach pains. They rushed him into surgery. He had a blockage in his bowel."

She stopped, but he knew there was more.

"What is it? Cancer?" He was aware that he sounded abrupt and harsh but was unable to do anything about it.

"Yes. The doctors said there was nothing they could do except make him comfortable."

He stared at her for a moment, then dropped his gaze to the scuffed toes of his boots.

So. The old man was finally on his way out. He was seventy-eight, so it was hardly surprising news. In fact, Tyler had been surprised he hadn't had a visit like this sooner—although he'd expected a lawyer, not a self-righteous elf.

He lifted his head. She was watching him, waiting for his response.

"Thanks for letting me know. I appreciate it." He walked past her, heading for the door to the showroom.

"Don't you want to know where he is so you can see him?" she called after him.

He kept walking. "No."

His father dying didn't change anything. Didn't even come close.

"You don't care that he's going to die alone? That there's no one to look after him? That he's living in a house filled with stacked-up newspapers and eating canned food?"

He stopped and turned to face her. She looked appalled. Shocked that anyone could be so cold. He almost smiled. Almost. His father had obviously done a great job convincing her he was a harmless, little old man. And who knew, maybe age had genuinely mellowed him.

Good for him.

"I said goodbye to my father years ago." He pushed the door open and walked into the showroom.

He half expected her to follow him. She'd been so full of fire and brimstone that he wouldn't have put it past her. He waited, muscles tense, but no one came through the door.

Good.

He strode through the showroom to the office. Gabby was going over a supplies manifest, one elbow on the desk, a fluorescent marker between her teeth.

"I thought you disconnected the old answering machine because it wasn't working?" he asked.

She blinked and he realized he'd barked the question instead of asking it like a normal person.

"Sorry," he muttered.

"What's wrong?"

"Nothing."

She gave him a long look. That was the problem with having his ex-girlfriend as his business manager—she knew him too well to let him get away with anything.

"Is there something wrong with the Crestwell account?" she asked.

"Everything's fine. Where's the old answering machine?"

"I told Dino to disconnect it. But if he didn't, it's where it always is."

She gestured to the far corner where a pile of boxes and files were stacked on a small coffee table, waiting to be returned to order after the flooding from the storm. Tyler hefted boxes out of the way until he'd unearthed the machine.

"It's still connected," he reported.

Gabby made a rude noise. "Bloody Dino. Talk about hopeless."

He pressed the blinking red light. "You have twenty new messages," an electronic voice told him.

"Shit," Gabby said.

He knew from experience that the machine only recorded twenty messages before it reached capacity. He wondered how many important calls they'd missed over the past few weeks.

The first three messages were customers with queries that he knew had long since been handled. He pressed the fast-forward button.

"Hey," Gabby said.

He saw she had a pen in hand and had been jotting down names and numbers as the messages played.

"You can go over them all later," he said.

"What's wrong with doing it now?"

He ignored her, letting the machine hit the end of the tape before rewinding to the last message.

"Hi. I'm calling for Tyler Adamson. My name's Ally Bishop. I'm living next door to his father, Bob, up here in Woodend. I thought Tyler would like to know that his father is in hospital. I think…I think it's pretty serious.…"

He hit the Stop button. Gabby was uncharacteristically silent behind him.

"Can you make sure we replace this thing today?" Tyler said, not turning around.

"Are you okay?"

He nodded.

"Do you want me to make some calls…?" Gabby offered.

"No."

"You don't want to go to him?"

He glanced at her over his shoulder. He and Gabby had gone out for three years, so she knew he never saw his father. But he'd never told her why.

"No."

"But—"

"Leave it, Gab."

He left the office and walked out into the workshop. Dino was on the lathe and Wes was sanding a tabletop, his face hidden behind safety goggles and a dust mask. Paul and Carl were marking up some wood. Kelly would be out the back somewhere, no doubt, checking on inventory or spraying something in the booth. Tyler breathed in the familiar smell of fresh-cut wood and varnish, then headed straight to the mezzanine where his work space was located. He sat in front of his drawing board and tried to lose himself in the design for a sideboard, but his head was full of old memories and feelings he'd thought long forgotten.

His father, red in the face, spittle flying from his mouth as he raged at Tyler for being insubordinate and useless.

His brother cowering beneath the lash of his father's belt while Tyler watched, filled with a mix of horror and shameful relief that this time it wasn't him on the receiving end of his father's wrath.

His mother, thin-lipped, telling him that he'd brought it on himself for being cheeky and rebellious.

Happy times, indeed.

Was it any wonder Tyler had escaped as soon as he could, following his brother's lead and bailing on school and home when he was barely seventeen? He'd left with nothing but a bag full of clothes and his father's angry "good riddance to bad rubbish," ringing in his ears—and he'd never looked back. Not once.

Sure, he'd visited when his mother was still alive, driven by guilt and obligation. But when she died ten years ago, he'd made a promise to himself to never go back, to put it all behind himself and never dredge it up again.

I think...I think it's serious.

Tyler swore beneath his breath. So what if his father was sick? So what if he was dying? Being closer to the grave didn't make him less of a bully and a coward, and it certainly didn't expunge seventeen years of violence and anger.

I think...I think it's serious.

"I can take care of those client briefings tomorrow if you need time off," Gabby said from the doorway.

Tyler glanced at her. She leaned against the door frame, her arms crossed beneath her small breasts, her brown eyes steady on him. She wore her hair short, like Ally Bishop, but it was straight instead of curly so she looked more boyish than puckish.

"I'm not going anywhere."

Gabby studied his face for a beat. "You never told me why you hate him so much."

"I don't hate him." That would give the old man too much power. "I don't want him in my life."

"I don't suppose there's any point in me offering an ear if you need to talk?" Gabby's tone was resigned and sad.

His refusal to talk about his childhood had been one of the major hurdles of their failed relationship. One of her favorite accusations had been that he was "emotionally withholding." Whatever that meant. Just because he wanted to leave the past in the past didn't mean he was holding anything back. It was simply irrelevant.

"There's nothing to talk about."

Gabby sighed. "Well. The offer stands if you want it."

"I appreciate it."

She pushed away from the door frame. "Just remember, you're only going to get this chance once, Tyler."

He nodded tightly. He'd had his fill of short, dark-haired women telling him what to do today.

"Gotcha."

He worked at his drawing board for the rest of the afternoon. By the time he descended from the mezzanine, the workshop was silent and the light was off in Gabby's office.

He did a quick lap of the building, checking doors, inspecting the pieces that had been put to one side ready for delivery, ensuring the machinery was all switched off.

Last year, T.A. Furniture Designs had turned over nearly four million dollars. This year, they were on track to increase that by 20 percent—despite the global economic downturn, despite a general slow-down in spending across the board. Years of hard work and commitment to quality craftsmanship and design were, at last, paying off and if things kept going the way they were, the company would outgrow their current premises in the next few years.

Not so useless, after all, hey, Dad?

He stopped in his tracks, hand poised to flick off the master light switch.

Everything in him wanted to deny that proving himself to his domineering father had been part of his motivation for building this business. It seemed such a childish, petty admission—as though his whole life had been one big "Look, Pa, no hands!"

But the truth was that whether Tyler liked it or not, there would always be a voice in his head telling him that he wasn't good enough and that he'd never amount to anything—and that voice was his father's.

He reached for his phone and hit the speed dial for Gabby.

"I need you to cover for me tomorrow," he said the moment she picked up.

To her credit, she didn't make a smug remark or say I told you so. She simply told him she'd make sure things were taken care of while he did what he had to do.

He stood for a long moment after he'd ended the call, thinking about what it would mean. Going home. Seeing his father again after ten years of silence.

He sighed. Then he flicked the light off and headed for the door.

WHAT AM I GOING TO TELL BOB?

The thought circled Ally Bishop's mind the entire drive to the small rural Victorian town of Woodend. True, she also spared a little time to fume over what a cold, unfeeling jerk Tyler Adamson was. But most of her thoughts were for the old man she was about to disappoint.

She was the one who had insisted Bob think about making contact with his estranged sons. She was the one who'd encouraged him to give his sons a chance to prove themselves, even though Bob had insisted they wouldn't care. And now she was the one who would have to deliver the cruel news that the one son she'd been able to track down wanted nothing to do with him, as Bob had so heartbreakingly predicted.

She still couldn't believe that Tyler had walked away from the news that his father was dying. That he didn't care. That it meant nothing to him that any last chance to reconcile or make his peace with his parent was about to disappear for good.

It wasn't as though she was one of those eternally optimistic people who only saw the best in people— her work as an advice columnist for Melbourne's most popular daily newspaper ensured that she was exposed to pretty much every peccadillo, flaw, peculiarity and weakness of human nature possible. In fact, she'd thought she was impossible to shock—until Tyler had coolly thanked her and walked away.

She glanced out the window as she passed the first houses on the outskirts of town. The turnoff to her friend Wendy's house came up on her left but Ally kept driving. Ten minutes later, she steered her car into a parking spot at the Kyneton District Hospital.

She didn't get out immediately. She needed a moment to gather herself for the task ahead.

According to Bob's doctors, his cancer was so widespread, so invasive, he had months, perhaps only weeks, to live. And she'd offered him hope. Now she was about to snatch that hope away from him.

She sighed heavily and scrubbed her face with her hands.

Not for the first time, she wondered how she had become so entangled so quickly in the concerns of an old man who, to all intents and purposes, was a stranger. After all, she'd only been living in Woodend for four weeks, house-sitting for Wendy. Prior to Bob's collapse, they'd only shared a couple of brief chats across the fence that separated the two properties. She hadn't even known his last name before he'd been admitted to hospital. And yet she'd taken on his cause as though it was her own.

Feeling about a million years old, she climbed out of the car and walked toward the hospital. Bob was dozing when she entered his ward, his face slack. She guessed he'd once been a strapping man—big boned, muscular—but age and illness had whittled him away, reducing him to little more than skin and bone and sinew. As always, his frailty made her chest squeeze with sympathy and she couldn't help flashing back to the awful, terrifying moment when she'd glanced over the fence and seen him sprawled unconscious on the grass. The twenty minutes she'd sat beside his too-still body, holding his hand while she waited for the ambulance to arrive had been the longest of her life.

Bob's eyelids flickered as she sank into the visitor's chair. His eyes opened and he blinked a few times before focusing on her. She smiled.

"Hello. How are you feeling?"

"I'll do."

Not once in all the turmoil and anxiety and uncertainty of the past few days had Bob let on that he was afraid of what his future held.

"Have you seen the doctor today?"

"He came by again. Wanted to make sure he'd given me enough of those little white pills to keep me well and truly off my rocker."

"Good. Because you don't need to be in pain."

Bob pulled a face. She was well aware that he came from a generation of Australian men who'd chop off an arm before they admitted a weakness.

"How are you doing with your crossword-puzzle books? Do you want me to get some more for you?"

"I'm fine for the moment, thanks, love."

Tell him. Tell him and get it over with.

Ally shifted to the edge of her seat. Took a steadying breath. "I spoke to Tyler today," she said.

Bob stilled. It was a moment before he responded. "Lazy bugger finally found the time to call, did he?"

Ally opened her mouth to explain that she'd confronted Tyler in person after he hadn't responded to her phone message, then thought better of it. Bob didn't need to know all the details, only the important ones. She could spare him that, at least.

"I don't think he's going to come, Bob," she said gently.

Bob's hands found each other on top of the sheet. Then he nodded. "No surprises there, I guess. Never did have time for the old man."

Only the muscle working at his jaw gave any hint that he was grappling with strong emotion.

She wondered again what had gone so wrong between Bob and his children, what words and deeds had been said and done to put so much distance between them. One thing was clear—Bob certainly wasn't about to volunteer the details. Which meant that Ally had done all she could to help him on that front.

"I'm sorry, Bob."

"Not your fault, love."

He asked about her column then and she pulled her latest letters from her bag and read him the juiciest problems. After fifteen minutes of offering her his pithy take on her readers' issues, Bob started to slur his words a little and she knew he was getting tired.

"I'll let you get some rest now. But I'll see you again tomorrow, okay?"

"You don't have to come in here every day. You've got your own things to do, all those letters to answer," Bob said.

"I'll see you tomorrow," Ally repeated with a small smile.

She kissed him on the cheek before exiting the room. She let the smile fade when she was in the corridor.

Feeling sad and heavy, she drove to Wendy's house. Mr. Whiskers wound himself around her ankles the moment she opened the front door and she took the hint and fed him immediately. Then she tried to settle down to get a start on tomorrow's column. Her mind kept drifting to Bob, however, unable to let go. She told herself over and over that Bob was not her responsibility, that she'd done all she could do. It didn't make any difference.

Ironic, really, since she'd spent practically all her adult life and much of her childhood ensuring she was as self-sufficient as possible. At thirty-three, she was a master at forming friendships that encompassed favors but not obligations, and relationships that offered companionship and passion without commitment or promises.

Yet here she was, worried and anxious over an old man she barely knew.

It's because he's so alone.

But at the end of the day, everyone was alone.

Shaking off her somber mood, Ally reapplied herself to solving other people's problems.

IT TOOK TYLER JUST OVER an hour to reach the outskirts of Woodend the following morning. He drove into Main Street, taking in the changes that ten years had wrought, a little surprised by how prosperous and lively it all seemed. There was fresh paint on shopfronts, more bustle along the sidewalks, new planter boxes and paving and a brand-spanking-new supermarket complex.

He frowned, struggling to reconcile the present with his memories of a town that had always seemed too grim and too small and too isolated. A town he couldn't wait to escape.

He drove farther north until he found the hospital. The morning sun was warm on his back as he strode toward the front entrance.

He had no idea what to expect. What to say to his father. How he would feel when he saw him for the first time in over a decade.

He'd told Gabby that he didn't hate his father, but he wasn't sure it was true. Once, he'd wanted his father's love and approval as much as any little boy. It had taken him a long time to accept that he would never hear the words of support and unconditional love that he craved. And longer than that again to understand that the fault wasn't with him, but with his father and, to a certain extent, his mother.

Just do it. See him. Listen to whatever he wants to say. Say your bit. Then it's over, once and for all.

He approached the reception desk, breathing in the medicinal smell shared by hospitals the world over, thinking about the phone conversation he'd had with Jon last night.

They weren't the closest of brothers. Even as kids they'd never discussed what went on within the four walls of their home. There had never seemed much point—their parents ruled their world, and there was nowhere else to go. So they'd endured, until one day when Jon was barely fourteen years old. He'd taken a hit from their father, but instead of curling into a ball to brace himself and endure the next inevitable blow, he'd gotten off the floor and squared up to the old man, both fists raised, his whole body trembling with rage. Tyler could still remember the shock and fear in his father's face as he'd realized his eldest son was taller than him. And the dawning anger as he understood that his days of ruling the roost with a casual cuff or kick were over.

Robert Adamson had never dared raise a hand to Jon after that and he was always careful to ensure his eldest son was out of the house before he laid into Tyler. A part of Tyler had wanted to hide behind his brother's newly found strength, to run to him and tell him what was still going on when he wasn't around. But the bulk of him had been too ashamed. Watching his brother stand his own ground had made him feel even smaller and less powerful and more trapped than he had before. It had taken Tyler many secretive sessions on the bench press at his friend Jimmy's house and hours of shadowboxing before he'd gotten the courage to stand his ground in the same way when he was thirteen years old. The beatings had stopped, but not the verbal abuse.

So perhaps it wasn't so surprising that Jon had sounded more cautious than pleased when he'd heard Tyler's voice over the phone last night. Family had never been associated with happiness for either of them. And when Tyler had revealed why he was calling, Jon had laughed outright.

"If that old bastard thinks I'm getting on a plane to play the dutiful son by his deathbed, he can think again," he'd said.

Tyler hadn't tried to talk him around. He'd done his bit, passed on the information. Jon had chosen his route, and Tyler his own. As always.

The woman behind the reception counter directed him to his father's ward. Tyler followed the signs and started counting off numbers as he looked for his father's room.

"Excuse me. Visiting hours don't start until ten."

He turned to find a gray-haired nurse walking toward him.

"I've driven up from Melbourne. I won't be long." It wouldn't take five minutes to say what he needed to say, after all.

"Who are you visiting?" the woman asked.

"Robert Adamson. My father." His throat closed around the unfamiliar word.

The nurse's expression softened. "Of course you are. I can see the family resemblance now. I'm Sister Kemp. Before you go in, can I grab some contact details from you? We don't seem to have them on file."

Tyler hesitated a moment. "Sure."

He followed her to the nurses' station then handed over his cell and home numbers.

"Lovely. I know our social worker will be pleased to know Bob has family looking out for him. You can go in to see him now, but keep it short. He's had major surgery and you'll find he tires very easily." She gave him a small smile before turning to take care of a ringing phone.

Tyler glanced toward the open doorway of his father's room. Then he realized he was hovering like an uncertain schoolboy and made himself move.

The moment he stepped over the threshold, he knew there had been some kind of a mistake. The small, white-haired figure sleeping in the hospital bed was not his father. Robert Adamson was broad shouldered and robust, with a full head of salt-and-pepper hair, not pallid and frail-looking, his features sunken, the pink of his skull showing through a thin covering of white hair.

Tyler took a step backward. Then the man in the bed stirred, his hands flexing briefly before relaxing again on the blanket. Tyler stilled. He knew those hands. Big, broad. Powerful.

Bloody hell.

He moved closer to the bed. How could this shrunken, diminished figure be his father, the man who loomed large and angry in all of Tyler's memories of his childhood? How could so much overbearing energy be reduced to this...?

Tyler eyed the tube snaking into the crook of his father's elbow and the oxygen prongs taped to his upper lip. There were more tubes disappearing beneath the blankets and a heart monitor kept up a steady *beep-beep* at the head of the bed.

How long had his father been so thin, the muscles of his arms so wasted? How long had his collarbone poked so obviously through his skin? What had happened to the square certainty of his jaw? The determined line of his brow?

Tyler swallowed against a wash of emotion. Amazing that after so many years and so much ill feeling he could feel anything, any tug of affection or sentiment at all. But this man was a part of him, a part of his marrow and blood and flesh and bone. He'd taught Tyler how to kick a football and hammer a nail. He'd sat at the head of the table every Sunday and carved the lamb roast. Even in his absence, he'd been the most influential person in Tyler's life.

His father.

"Tyler."

Tyler's gaze snapped to his father's face and he saw that he was awake, his pale blue eyes defiant and proud as he stared at his son.

"That's right."

"Thought you were too busy down there in the city with your little furniture business to have time for your old man."

Typical of his father to come out fighting. It was a painless jab, but it was enough to give Tyler some much-needed perspective. This man—this old, frail man—was not his mentor or his friend. Never had been, never would be.

"We're flat out, actually. So I can't stay long."

"Nobody asked you to." His parent smoothed a hand over his hair. "Did you talk to Jon?"

"I did." He didn't say anything more and his father was the first to look away.

"Well, it's a long way to come from Canada. I assume he's still over there, freezing his nuts off every winter?"

"That's right."

"Wife and kids?" his father asked hopefully.

"No."

"How about you?"

"No."

His father looked disappointed. Tyler glanced around the room, trying to think of something else to say. There were no cards or flowers on the bed stand, but someone had brought his father some crossword-puzzle books. His father shifted in the bed, then winced and subsided back on his pillows.

"You okay?"

"Does it look like I'm okay?" In the old days, his father's words would have been delivered with scathing contempt, just in case Tyler hadn't got the message over the past thirty-seven years that his father found him lacking on almost every front. There was no weight or vehemence behind today's utterance, however—it was simply a reflex, the last remnant of a lifelong habit.

"What are your plans?" Tyler asked.

His father glared at him. "What do you mean, what are my plans? I've got a handful of weeks left. I wasn't planning on a fishing expedition."

Tyler regarded him for a long, silent moment. It was hard to get angry or even irritated when he could see how much effort it was taking his father to maintain his usual brusque demeanor. Robert Adamson was a toothless tiger, a declawed lion, a gelded stallion. Whatever power he once wielded in the world was long gone.

"What have the doctors said?"

"Why? Wondering how soon you can get your hands on the house?"

"I don't need your money, Dad," Tyler said, then cursed himself for rising to the bait.

He took a deep breath. He hadn't come here to fight. He'd come to say his piece, and the sooner he did that, the sooner he could get back to his life.

He opened his mouth to deliver the speech he'd prepared in the small hours of the morning—sharp, brutal words designed to severe the ties between them at last. Then he looked into his father's watery blue eyes and saw past the surface pride to the well of fear and uncertainty beneath.

The words he'd waited years to say died in his throat.

The man lying before him had only weeks, maybe

a handful of months left. No matter how much he deserved it, no matter how many times Tyler had imagined himself looking his father in the eye and listing his father's failures as a parent and a man, he could not make himself say the words sitting like lead in his belly.

He simply couldn't.

Some of the tension eased out of his shoulders.

So. That was that, then. He'd say his goodbyes and walk away and leave the big issues between them unexplored, as they always had been. Let the old man slip away without nailing him with the questions he'd always wanted answers to.

What did we do wrong?

Did you ever love us?

Why even have children if you resented them so deeply?

"I need to go," Tyler said. He dug his car keys from his pocket. "Is there anything you need before I head off? Anything from home? Something from the shop?"

"I'm all covered. Ally brought me my things."

Right. Ally, the next-door neighbor. It sounded like the kind of thing a self-righteous elf would do.

"Then I'd best be getting back to it," Tyler said.

His father nodded as though he'd expected nothing less. "Appreciate you dropping by."

Tyler headed for the door, an odd, sick feeling in his gut.

He'd just said goodbye to his father for the last

time. Once he returned to Melbourne, that would be it. It would all be over.

Impossible to untangle all the thoughts and feelings racing through his mind. Regret, anger, grief, frustration. And, yes, pity.

He strode through the corridors, dodging patients and medical staff. Then he exited the hospital—and almost walked straight into a small, dark-haired woman.

They both stopped in their tracks. For a moment, Ally Bishop simply stared at him. Then a wide smile curved her mouth.

"You came," she said. "I'm so glad. I know he really wanted to see you. He's so proud and stubborn, but the moment I mentioned calling you I could see he wanted it, he simply didn't know how to ask for it."

She was delighted he'd come. Overjoyed by the family reunion she'd effected. No doubt she had visions of him and his father staying up late into the night, exchanging memories, sharing their innermost thoughts. Telling each other how proud they were and how much they loved each other.

He laughed. Couldn't help himself.

"Lady, you have no idea," he said.

He left her standing in front of the hospital, her face pale with shock.

He made it to the safety of his truck before it all caught up with him. He pinched the bridge of his nose but was powerless to stop the tears burning the back of his eyes.

They're not for him. They're not.

He wasn't sure who he was crying for. Definitely not his old man, and certainly not himself. He'd never cried for himself, and he wasn't about to start now.

CHAPTER TWO

I'VE MADE A TERRIBLE mistake.

Ally's hand curled around the strap of her handbag as she watched Tyler Adamson duck his head and brush his forearm across his eyes.

She'd followed him to his truck, determined to make the most of his change of heart despite his less-than-welcoming demeanor. After all, he'd come when he said he wouldn't—that had to mean there was a chance of father and son reconciling.

But now Tyler was hunched in his truck, choking back tears as though they caused him physical pain.

At first she'd thought it was simple grief she was witnessing, that Tyler had seen his father and learned the prognosis and was now experiencing the first wash of sorrow and regret. But there was something about the way he curled into himself that spoke of emotions more complex and uglier than grief alone.

She took a step backward, then another, then another, until there was a tree between herself and Tyler's shiny red pickup. She turned and walked until she was safely inside the hospital foyer, well out of Tyler's sight.

With the abruptness of a camera changing focus, she suddenly understood that she should never have made contact with him. Should never have pushed Bob, should never have pried into what was clearly a very complicated, painful situation. She'd thought she was helping, that if there were issues between Bob and his children, they would all appreciate the opportunity to talk them out before it was too late.

But some scars ran too deep and she'd been hopelessly, childishly naive to dive headfirst into something that was clearly none of her business. She'd been behaving like the worst sort of interfering do-gooder, lumbering in with her hobnail boots on, causing everyone more pain.

She wrapped her arms across herself as she glanced toward the parking lot, feeling cold despite the warmth of the summer's day. She couldn't get the picture of Tyler hunched over his steering wheel out of her mind. She knew instinctively that he would hate for her—for anyone—to have seen him in such a vulnerable state.

The worst of it was, there was nothing she could do to fix the mess she'd made. She'd meddled, and there was no way she could take it back.

And now Ally was uncertain if she should go ahead with her visit or not, unsure what she might find when she entered Bob's room. If he was as upset as his son, she knew absolutely that he would not want anyone to see him break down.

She bit her lip. Then she gave herself a mental shake. She was here. If Bob didn't want to see her, she'd go. And if he was upset, she'd do her best to comfort him—provided he allowed her to. It was the least she could do.

Bob was talking to a nurse when she arrived. Or, more accurately, arguing, judging by the raised voices.

"Fine, Mr. Adamson, I'll go find someone in charge," the nurse said darkly, brushing past Ally as she exited the room.

Bob was scowling as Ally approached the bed. "She'd better be going to find someone to make this TV work, or there's going to be hell to pay."

"What's the problem, Bob?"

"They want to stiff me to watch my TV shows. Twenty bucks a day!"

"It's been like that for a while. Do you want me to arrange it for you?"

"No, I do not. It's an outrage to charge a man to watch what should be free." He was flushed, agitated—far more so than the argument warranted.

Ally reached for one of the gnarled hands fisted on the sheets. "Bob, you need to take a deep breath. Getting upset like this isn't going to help you get better."

He didn't quite meet her eyes but his hand gripped hers tightly, almost painfully.

"I guess you probably think I'm a stupid old bugger, getting upset over a TV." His voice was low, thick with emotion. She returned the pressure on his hand.

"Actually, I don't."

Then she set herself to the task of distracting him, telling him a story about Wendy's cat, Mr. Whiskers. She waited for him to mention his son's visit, but he didn't. And neither did she.

She'd learned her lesson, well and truly.

TYLER HESITATED ON THE rear doorstep of his father's house, the spare key gritty with dirt and cool in his hand. It had been hidden beneath the old brick beside the steps for as long as he could remember, but he'd still been surprised when he'd lifted the brick and found it there. For some reason he'd thought his father would have changed the hiding spot after he and Jon had left.

He rubbed his thumb over the ridges on the key, staring at the peeling paint of the door.

He didn't know why he was here. He'd been driving through town on his way to the freeway, keen to get back to the business, his head busy with all the things he needed to do between now and the weekend. Then he'd seen the sign for his parents' street and signaled to turn.

Like his father, the house hadn't aged well. The paint was peeling, and the trim around several of the window frames was rotten. The garden was overgrown, the gutters sagging along one side of the house.

The key slid easily into the lock. The door swung open and a rush of hot, stale air hit him. He walked into the short hallway, stopping when he saw the boxes stacked against the wall. More than a dozen of them, filled with what looked like newspapers. He took a step closer and inspected the topmost one.

Yep, newspapers. So old they were yellow with age. Frowning, he made his way past the cartons and into the kitchen.

It was dark and he reached for the light switch. Even after twenty years he found it unerringly, some subconscious part of his brain leading his hand to the right point on the kitchen wall. The fluorescent light flickered to life and he surveyed the room, his frown deepening as he took note of yet more newspapers stacked against the wall, the dirty dishes in the sink, the food-encrusted stove.

When his mother had been alive, this room had been pristine, every surface clear, every pot gleaming. It had been his and Jon's responsibility to wash and dry and put away the dishes every night, then his mother would set the table for tomorrow's breakfast, everything neatly lined up.

He glanced toward the crowded sink and a memory hit—him and Jon fooling around while doing the dishes, flicking each other with their damp tea towels. He'd been holding one of his mother's prized Royal Doulton teacups when he'd slipped on the wet floor and instinctively flailed to save himself, dropping the cup in the process. The sound of porcelain shattering had sounded like a gunshot through the house. Tyler could still remember the thrill of panic that had rocketed up his spine.

His mother had appeared in the doorway first, her face twisted with dismay and grief, then his father. One look at his wife's tear-streaked face as she'd knelt to collect the remains of one of her treasured teacups had been enough to seal Tyler's fate.

Tyler walked away from the memory and into the living room. The curtains were drawn, the room dark, and he flicked on more lights. Apart from the cartons of newspapers stacked along the far wall, nothing had changed in here since he'd last seen it, down to his mother's knitting basket sitting beside her favorite chair by the fire.

He crossed to the mantle and picked up a tiny porcelain mouse peering out of a piece of cheese. His mother had loved her menagerie, as she'd called it. He and Jon had selected a new animal for her birthday every year, bought from the jeweler in town and paid for with their hard-earned pocket money. She'd always acted surprised when she'd opened her present, even though she must have known she'd be getting yet another creature to add to her collection.

Tyler traced the line of the mouse's back, remembering how proud he'd always been of the fact that he'd made her happy, even for a moment.

He put down the mouse and glanced toward the

bedrooms. He walked slowly across the threadbare carpet and stepped into the empty hallway. Closed doors lined the right side, the first leading to his parents' room, the next to Jon's, the last to his. At the far end of the hall was the door to the bathroom.

Tyler reached out to flick on the light switch and another memory flashed into his mind. Jon, naked and still wet from the shower, cowering on the carpet as their father lit into him with an old belt. Jon had tried to escape to his room and their father had stalked him up the hallway, raining blows on his exposed back. Tyler had stood in his bedroom door, too afraid to intervene, too afraid to retreat.

Tyler couldn't remember what his brother's crime had been. Perhaps he'd been in their father's toolbox without permission. Maybe he'd sat in their father's car, pretending he could drive, a favorite fantasy for both him and Jon. Or maybe he'd genuinely done something wrong—lied or stolen or cheated at school.

Tyler could feel his heart beating against his rib cage. He glanced around, feeling overwhelmed by the gloom and the smell of old papers and the memories. So much ugliness and sadness.

He'd intended to check out his old room, but instead he turned and grabbed the nearest carton of newspapers. Hefting it, he strode to the entrance and balanced the box on his knee while he opened the front door. Then he strode down the steps and dumped the box by the curb.

He stared at the yellowed newspaper for a beat, then he turned on his heel and went into the house. He crossed into the living room and jerked the curtains open, letting in bright, clean light. He slid the catches free and pushed the window open. He did the same thing with the other window, then he walked into the kitchen and wound the blinds up and pushed that window wide, too.

He returned to the hall, grabbed another box and headed for the curb.

ALLY STOPPED BY THE supermarket on the way home. She was just adding the latest edition of *Country Living* magazine to her shopping basket when she glanced up and saw a familiar blonde head.

"Daniel," she said automatically, taking a step forward.

Immediately she felt ridiculous, because Daniel was in London, thousands of miles away.

The man looked over his shoulder and she murmured an apology. Ducking her head, she made her way to the checkout.

It wasn't the first time she'd thought she'd seen Daniel on the street or in the supermarket. She understood it was guilt, that she still hadn't forgiven herself for leaving and hurting him the way she had. As she paid for her groceries and made her way to her car, she told herself the same thing she always did—she'd done him a kindness in the long-term.

She wondered if he understood that yet.

It's been five years, Bishop. You're probably a faded memory, if that. He's probably married with three kids and a huge mortgage by now.

Strange that the thought made her throat tight when it was everything she knew she didn't want.

She drove home, drowning her thoughts with the car radio. She slowed when she turned onto her street and saw a shiny red pickup parked in her usual spot under the tree.

Tyler's truck, unless she was wildly mistaken. She parked behind him, glancing toward Bob's place. For the first time since she'd been living next door, the curtains were all open, the windows thrown wide. Out the front, half a dozen cardboard boxes were stacked along the curb.

She'd only been in Bob's house twice, once to call the ambulance when he'd collapsed, the second to collect his pajamas and crossword puzzles to make him more comfortable in hospital. Both times she'd been dismayed by the dark rooms and stacks of newspaper and the evidence that he'd been living off canned food and little else. She'd literally itched to do something about all of it—but it hadn't been her place and she'd satisfied herself with disposing of any perishables in the fridge and taking out the garbage.

She gathered her groceries, locked the car and started toward Wendy's front gate. She was fumbling with the latch when she heard heavy footsteps drum on the ancient planks of Bob's porch. Seconds later,

Tyler appeared, a box of newspapers in his arms as he strode up the garden path. He was frowning and his dark hair was ruffled as though he'd been running his fingers through it. He pushed Bob's gate open with his knee, then crossed to the curb. His big biceps muscles bulged as he dropped the box on top of the others. He turned and registered her for the first time.

She felt an odd thud in the pit of her stomach when she met his gaze. She'd been preoccupied during their previous meetings, but in the clear midday light she was struck by the unusual color and clarity of his cool silver-gray eyes.

"Hi," she said.

He nodded his head in silent acknowledgment. Then he headed into the house.

"Wait!"

He paused, one hand on the gate, eyebrows raised, his body angled only slightly toward her.

Not exactly welcoming or encouraging. But she probably deserved not to be welcomed or encouraged, the way she'd lumbered into his life with her preconceived judgments and inexcusable meddling.

"I just wanted to say I was sorry. For yesterday, I mean. I made a lot of judgments based on not a lot of information and it was really out of line for me to read you the riot act the way I did." Her words came out a little rushed, but at least she'd said them.

It took him a moment to respond, and she realized she'd surprised him.

"Don't worry about it."

"But—"

"You were being a good neighbor. I get it."

"Well, yes, but I was also being a horrible busy-body. I get about a hundred letters a week from people making exactly the same mistake, so you'd think I'd know better, but apparently I don't. Apparently I'm as susceptible to do-gooder syndrome as the next person." She offered him a small, self-deprecating smile.

His gaze slid down her body briefly before coming back to her face.

"You're a psychologist?"

She wasn't sure if she should be insulted by the skepticism in his tone or not.

"I'm an advice columnist. I write the Dear Gertrude column in the *Melbourne Herald.*"

"Right." He didn't seem very impressed with her profession.

"I see you're having a bit of a clear out," she said, gesturing toward the stacks near the curb.

"Those newspapers are a fire hazard."

There was a preemptive defensiveness to his tone and she guessed that Bob had no idea he was about to lose his newspaper collection.

"Well. Good luck with it," she said. "I hope everything works out okay." She offered him another smile before pushing Wendy's gate open. Once she was safely inside the house, she closed her eyes and groaned.

I hope everything works out okay.

There was only one way things were going to work out. Bob was dying. There was no miracle happy ending to this story.

Rolling her eyes at herself, she carried the groceries to the kitchen and started putting them away.

She'd handled that really well. Not.

She tried to concentrate on work for the rest of the afternoon but it was almost impossible to ignore all the activity next door. Now that the curtains and blinds were open at Bob's house, she had a ringside view into both the kitchen and living room from her customary perch at Wendy's desk in the study. She saw Tyler moving back and forth and back and forth as he worked at clearing Bob's hoard of newspapers. She heard him swear a few times, heard him talking on his phone, his deep voice drifting through the window in indecipherable snatches.

By three, she'd chosen only one letter for her next column and she shut the letters file on her computer with a frustrated sigh. Clearly she was too distracted—unsettled—to work properly. She might as well call it quits for the day.

She logged on to the internet instead and spent the next few hours checking out the latest offerings on her favorite house-sitting site.

She'd been house-sitting for nearly three years now and had a solid history to offer prospective clients, so there was a pretty good chance she had a shot at any job she applied for. Typically, no actual money changed hands—the homeowners provided the accommodation, she ensured their properties and gardens and pets remained in good order. A you-scratch-my-back-and-I'll-scratch-yours kind of deal. To date, the longest span she'd had between jobs was three weeks, and a serviced apartment had provided the necessary stopgap. As far as she was concerned, it was the perfect lifestyle choice, a great solution for a born-and-bred gypsy.

She bookmarked two options that had possibilities—one in Sydney, the other in Brisbane—then shut down the computer and went into the kitchen to stuff and baste the chicken she'd bought for dinner. She could see Tyler moving around Bob's kitchen on the other side of the fence. She watched out of the corner of her eye as he tackled the dishes before turning his attention to the stovetop and oven. Clearly, he was as appalled as she'd been by the way his father had been living.

She frowned as she slid the chicken into the oven. She couldn't work Tyler out. When she'd first accosted him in Melbourne, she'd gained the impression that there was no love lost between father and son. Then he'd shown up at the hospital, and there had been that moment in the parking lot. And now he was clearing out his father's house…

Did we or did we not decide that this was absolutely none of our business and that we'd already grossly overstepped the line with our interfering?

Tearing her gaze from Bob's window, she turned to

grab the tray of potatoes and added them to the oven. Then she settled down to kill an hour with *Country Living* magazine and lots of lovely house interiors.

By seven, the house was filled with the smell of chicken and garlic potatoes. Her stomach rumbled as she put on greens to cook and whisked up some gravy. A bead of sweat trickled down her back and she used her forearm to push her damp hair off her forehead. Roasting a chicken probably hadn't been the smartest choice for such a warm day. She flipped on the air conditioner, then moved to the oven.

Her hands in oven mitts, she grasped the hot pan and pulled the chicken toward herself. The top was golden brown and crispy and she could smell the sage in the stuffing.

"Yum," she murmured.

Suddenly the world went dark.

Ally blinked, aware of the absolute silence around her—no hum from the fridge, no quiet whir from the oven or the air conditioner.

She'd blown a fuse. Damn.

The heat from the roasting pan was starting to burn through the mitts. She pushed the pan forward carefully until she felt it slide into the oven.

She had no idea if Wendy had a flashlight or not, but there was no way she was going to find it in the pitch-black. Arms extended in front of her, she fumbled to the study, where she'd left her phone. The screen came to life when she touched it and she used the light to guide her to the front door. She was pretty sure she'd seen a fuse box on the porch beside the door, the old-fashioned kind with a hinged wooden cover...

And there it was. *Phew*.

She found the catch and opened the cover, squinting in the feeble light from her phone as she tried to read the writing on the various fuses. This wasn't like the more modern trip-switch fuse boxes she was used to in the city. This was old school, with big ceramic plugs and what looked like fuse wire.

"Problem?" a voice asked out of nowhere.

She let out a little yelp and started so violently she nearly dropped the phone.

She pressed her free hand to her chest as she glanced over her shoulder. Tyler stood at the front gate, his face a study in shadows in the dim streetlight.

"You scared me," she said stupidly.

"No kidding." His tone was very dry. He gestured toward the fuse box. "Looks like you've blown something."

"I think I overloaded it having the air conditioner and oven on at the same time."

"Happens sometimes with these old places."

"I don't suppose you have a flashlight I could borrow?" she asked hopefully.

He didn't respond, simply turned on his heel and walked toward his pickup. Twenty seconds later, he pushed open Wendy's gate, a strong flashlight beam bouncing along the path in front of him.

Maybe it was because it was dark, but he seemed much bigger than she remembered as he climbed the two steps to the porch and stopped in front of her. She fought a ridiculous urge to take a step backward.

"Thanks for this. I really appreciate it," she said, holding out her hand for the flashlight.

He ignored her, brushing past her to aim the flashlight beam at the fuses.

She frowned. "I don't want to take up your time."

She made a policy of trying to solve her own problems without relying on the kindness of strangers. It was something she'd learned early in life.

"This fuse box is pretty old," he said.

"I'm sure I can work it out."

He glanced at her, his expression unreadable. "Don't tell me you're one of those feminists."

"'Fraid so. I'm happy to borrow a flashlight, but I'm not a damsel in distress."

He regarded her a moment, then he shrugged and passed her the flashlight. She waited for him to leave, but he simply stood to one side and waved a hand, inviting her into the prime position in front of the box.

"Thank you," she said, not feeling very grateful. She didn't particularly want to fumble around in front of him. Especially when she'd made such a big deal about fending for herself.

She aimed the flashlight, trying to appear as though she knew what she was doing. According to her sketchy memory of how these old systems worked, she was supposed to pull the fuses out to check which one had a broken wire. She reached to check the first one.

"It won't be that one. That's your lighting."

He had a shoulder against the house, his arms crossed over his chest. He looked as though he was enjoying himself.

"It's worth checking them all," she said stubbornly.

"If it makes you feel better."

She grit her teeth and pulled the fuse out. The wire was noticeably still intact and she plugged it in without comment.

"All good?"

"Yes," she said grudgingly. Maybe she would have been better off fumbling around for a candle and going to bed early after all.

"Only five more to go," he said encouragingly.

She shone the flashlight in his face.

"Smugness is really not an attractive trait, you know."

He pushed her hand down so that the beam was angled toward his chest.

"Neither is stubbornness."

They stared at each other a moment, neither giving an inch. Then she sighed and passed him the flashlight.

"Okay. Help me if you must."

"Only because you asked so nicely."

Instantly she felt rude and stupid. He'd come to

her aid, and instead of thanking him she was coming across as a prickly ingrate.

"Sorry. I guess I'm used to fending for myself."

"I can tell. Excuse me."

He moved closer to the fuse box and she took a hasty step backward, but not before she'd bumped against his hard shoulder. He'd been working all afternoon in the heat and he smelled of deodorant and clean sweat. Intensely masculine.

She crossed her arms over her chest. "What do you think it is?" she asked.

"There's a main fuse in here, usually it takes a higher gauge wire than the others..." He pulled a fuse out and inspected it. "Yeah."

"It's that one?"

"Yeah. You've overloaded the main."

"Stupid roasted chicken."

"It was probably the air conditioner."

"Can you fix it?"

"Depends."

He shone the flashlight around the fuse box, then ran his hand along the top shelf. He came away with nothing but dust and cobwebs.

"No spare fuse wire."

"Right." She thought for a minute. "The shops are probably already closed. So I guess that means I'm having an early night."

She spared a thought for the food in Wendy's freezer. Maybe if she didn't disturb it overnight, it wouldn't spoil.

"Hang on a moment."

She was left blinking in the darkness as Tyler left the porch and headed next door. She guessed he was checking his father's place for spare wire and she crossed her fingers. She watched Tyler expectantly as he climbed the steps to rejoin her. He didn't say a word, simply held up a small piece of card with fine wire wrapped around it.

"Bless you, Bob," she said fervently.

"Yeah." There was a dry undertone to the single word and she was reminded of the scene she'd witnessed this morning at the hospital.

Hard to imagine this big, capable man reduced to tears. But he had been. He'd been profoundly affected by his visit to his father.

"Can you hold the light steady for me?"

She trained the beam on his hands as he threaded new wire into the fuse. She took the opportunity to study his profile. He had a bump in his nose as though maybe he'd broken it at some stage, and a strong, square jaw. His dark hair was short and rumpled, and whiskers shadowed the lower half of his face. She could discern a thin scar on his cheekbone, below the corner of his left eye. She wondered how he'd gotten it. Fighting? A car accident?

She'd thought he was focused on the fuse, but he glanced up suddenly and his gaze locked with hers. She looked away quickly, feeling her face heat with embarrassment.

Busted, big-time.

"You might want to turn the air-conditioning off before I turn the power back on. Just in case," he said.

"Right. Of course."

She slipped into the house, feeling her way along the wall with one arm extended. She was only steps from the kitchen when her shin connected with something hard and heavy.

"Shit!" she hissed, bending to rub her aching shin.

"All right in there?" Tyler called.

"Yeah."

She reached out a hand and felt the lumpy metal outline of Wendy's umbrella stand. She stepped around it and entered the kitchen. She found the wall switch to turn off the air-conditioning, then crossed to the oven and turned that off for good measure. Then she made her way back to the porch.

"Houston, we are cleared to launch."

"Roger that." He plugged in the fuse and flipped the switch. She gave a little cheer as Wendy's cottage came back to life.

"Just like magic."

"Something like that."

He switched off the flashlight and collected his father's wire before shutting the fuse box.

"You should probably get an electrician in to update this setup," he said. "With a modern fuse, you'd only have to flip a switch to reset the power."

"I'll get on to it." She made a mental note to

mention it to Wendy during their next Skype chat. "I really appreciate your help."

"No worries." He started down the porch steps.

She watched his broad shoulders as he walked toward the gate, wondering if he ever waxed eloquent about anything.

Probably not. He struck her as being the strong, silent type.

"Have you eaten?" she called after him.

For the second time that day, he stopped and glanced over his shoulder at her.

"Sorry?"

"Have you eaten? I have a whole roast chicken inside and, even at my piggiest, I couldn't possibly eat it all…"

He hesitated, a slight frown forming between his eyebrows.

"Think of it as a barter, a drumstick in return for the loan of your flashlight and expertise," she said. "There are potatoes, too, and gravy."

She wasn't sure why she trying so hard to convince him. If he wasn't hungry, he wasn't hungry.

"Chicken sounds good. Give me a moment to wash up."

He disappeared through the front gate before she could say anything.

She returned to the kitchen and grabbed a second plate. The chicken hadn't had time to cool, but she set the heat beneath the greens on high to bring them back to the boil. The water was starting to bubble when she heard footsteps on the porch.

"Come in," she called.

His hair was damp and he was holding a six-pack of beer in one hand when he appeared in the doorway.

"Dad doesn't run to wine, I'm afraid."

"Beer's perfect. Although I have wine if you want it."

"I'll stick with the beer, thanks. Got to drive to Melbourne tonight."

"Sure."

She served the meal, very aware of him watching her every move. She paused when she was about to pour the gravy. Being a gravy lover, she liked it everywhere, but some people weren't so fond. "You like a little or a lot?" she asked.

"A lot. Can't have too much of a good thing."

A very vivid, very earthy image popped into her mind. She concentrated on pouring the sauce over his chicken and vegetables but she could feel heat climbing into her cheeks again.

Two blushes in twenty minutes. Apparently she was turning into a born-again virgin in her old age.

Get a grip, Bishop. Anyone would think you'd never had a meal with a man before.

"We can eat outside or in here."

"It'll be cooler outside," he said.

"Outside it is, then."

She led the way through the French doors and

onto the deck. They settled on opposite sides of the table. He twisted the top off a beer and placed it in front of her, then did the same for himself while she distributed the cutlery.

"Well," she said. "Enjoy."

She sliced off some chicken and potato and took a bite. He did the same and there was a short silence as they both chewed.

"You're a pretty good cook for a feminist."

She choked on her mouthful.

He gave her an innocent look. "Sorry. Was that politically incorrect?"

She reached for her beer and took a big swallow. Then she pointed the neck of her bottle at him.

"You're lucky I'm not one of those gun-toting members of the sisterhood or you'd be in big trouble right now."

"Would I?" His eyes crinkled at the corners as he looked at her.

Apparently Tyler found her amusing. Which was a little disconcerting, since she'd just made a rather startling discovery—he was a very attractive man. Somehow she'd managed to overlook that fact until now. With his dark hair and unusual silver-gray eyes, that bump in his nose and the decisive shape of his jaw and forehead, he was easily the best-looking man she'd shared a meal with in a long time.

Then there was his body.

Broad, hard, lean, with the kind of muscles that

came from doing things in the real world rather than pumping iron in the gym.

She dragged her gaze from him and concentrated on her meal, suddenly very aware of the fact that she'd pulled on her cowboy-and-Indian pajama pants when she came home from the supermarket and that she wasn't wearing a scrap of makeup.

Not exactly femme-fatale material.

Not that she was in the market to slay any man with her charms, such as they were, but a woman had her pride.

"So, how does a person become an advice columnist?" he asked.

"By accident. I was doing a column on travel destinations and they needed someone to fill in for Dear Gertrude when the writer who'd been doing it for years got sick. I did it for a couple of weeks, she decided to retire and they offered me the gig."

"You said your column's in the *Herald,* right?" he asked.

"Yup." It was also syndicated to a bunch of other papers, but he didn't need to know that.

"So people write in and tell you about all their problems and you solve them?"

"People write in with *a* problem and I attempt to offer them my objective opinion. Sometimes an outsider's point of view gives people a new perspective."

"I suppose you tell all your women readers to change their own tires and tote their own luggage?"

"You know, I do. I happen to be a big believer in personal responsibility. How about you?"

A slow grin spread across his face and she realized she'd risen to his bait without blinking. "Enjoying yourself?" she asked.

He made a show of stopping to think about it. "The chicken is good."

"Thank you."

"The beer is cold."

"Kudos to Bob."

"And you do rise to the bait pretty quickly."

She narrowed her eyes. "You're one of those people who think practical jokes are funny, aren't you?"

"Guilty as charged, Your Honor."

She couldn't hide her smile. No way would she have ever guessed that the man she'd confronted yesterday and run into this morning was capable of lighthearted teasing.

"So how does a person become a furniture designer?"

He shrugged and took a mouthful of his beer. "He's crap at math and English and science and he wants to leave school as quickly as possible."

She blinked at the harshness of his self-assessment. "Well, you clearly did something right."

"I know how to work hard. And I was lucky enough to have a great boss when I finally scored an apprenticeship. Taught me everything I know."

She studied the man sitting across from her. He was modest almost to the point of self-denigration, yet he was clearly a driven person. She'd seen his workshop in Melbourne—no one could build a business the size of T.A. Furniture Design without having a fire in their belly and the smarts to harness it. She was confused by the apparent contradiction. All the self-made, driven men she'd met had been egomaniacs, more than happy to shove their achievements down the throat of anyone who was stupid enough to inquire.

It made her wonder, which in turn made her think about Bob and all she knew, and didn't know, about her neighbor and his son.

None of your business, Bishop. Remember?

"Do you want another beer?" she asked, noticing his bottle was empty.

"No, thanks."

She went to collect a second bottle for herself, bringing him a glass of water.

"Thanks."

She racked her brain for a safe topic of conversation. Obviously, Bob was out. Too many pitfalls and unknowns there.

"There's ice cream for dessert," she said after a short silence.

Not exactly a sparkling conversational gambit, but a nice neutral topic nonetheless.

"Yeah?" There was an arrested look in Tyler's eyes. "What flavor?"

"Honey macadamia and New York Cheesecake."

"That's got to be Charmaine's," he said, naming

one of Melbourne's smaller boutique ice cream manufacturers.

She was impressed. "You know your ice creams."

The reason she knew this was because she, too, knew her ice creams. In fact, she had what her friends commonly referred to as a substance-abuse problem where the stuff was concerned.

"Have you tried their chili chocolate?" he asked.

"Yes. Have you tried the Peanut Nutter at Trampoline?" she asked, naming another ice cream parlor.

"Of course. But it's not as good as the cookies-and-cream gelati at this little place—"

"Near the corner of Rathdowne and Lygon streets in Carlton," she finished for him.

He sat back in his chair. "You know about Rafael's."

"I do."

"So if I say the words *almond biscotti*..."

"I'd know you were talking about Antica Gelateria del Corso, flagship store on Collins Street in the city."

They eyed each other for a speculative beat, then spoke simultaneously.

"Favorite flavor ever?"

They both laughed. Ally felt a little pinch low in her belly as she looked into his smiling face. Brooding and taciturn, this man was attractive. Laughing, he about took her breath away.

"You first," he said.

"Hmm..." She propped an elbow on the table while she pondered, very aware of her pulse tripping away at a faster than normal rate. "I'm going to go small and exclusive and homemade. My friend Craig made chocolate-and-lavender ice cream for my birthday last year. I swear, it was a religious experience."

"Full cream?"

"Double cream. Couverture chocolate. French lavender. I ate so much I was sick. The kicker is that he didn't write down the recipe, just threw stuff into the ice cream maker."

"It was a one-off?"

"For one night only." She sat back and crossed her legs. "Your turn."

His gaze drifted beyond her shoulder as he thought it over. She took a mouthful of beer. A warm breeze tickled the back of her neck and the cicadas sang to each other, their music a constant in the background.

"There's this place in Florence," he said after a short silence.

"Italy? You're pulling out the big guns. Going international on me."

His mouth quirked at the corner. "I am. This place is down a little cobbled street, hard to find. They only use fresh ingredients, so their sorbets are seasonal."

"I love a good sorbet."

"The sorbets are good, but they make this amazing

orange cake gelati… It's like eating a piece of orange poppy seed cake. Only better."

"Because it's ice cream."

"Yes."

There was a moment of contemplative, reverential silence. Then Ally laughed and fanned herself with her hand.

"Wow. I almost need a cigarette after that."

A slow grin curled his mouth. For a moment she forgot how and why they'd met, forgot that he'd spent the day clearing out his father's house, and that she'd held his father's hand at the hospital this morning. It was a warm, balmy night and she had alcohol warming the pit of her stomach and the world seemed ripe with possibilities.

It was just her, and him.

The sound of a phone ringing cut through the loaded silence. She blinked, and Tyler reached for his hip pocket.

"Sorry. It's probably work."

He flipped his phone open and took the call.

"Tyler speaking."

It was impossible to miss the way his face and body tensed as he listened to his caller.

"But he's okay now?"

She stilled. It had to be the hospital.

"I understand. Do you need me to come down there?"

She gripped the edge of the table. Surely Bob hadn't…?

"So he'll probably sleep through the night now?"

She relaxed a notch. Bob was alive, then. But clearly something was going on.

Tyler half turned away from her and she stacked their plates, then took them inside to give him some privacy.

She fussed in the kitchen, banging dishes and roasting pans to let him know she wasn't eavesdropping. She was taking the lids off the ice cream tubs when Tyler entered. His gaze took in the bowls on the counter as he slid his phone into his hip pocket.

"I might take a pass on dessert, if you don't mind. There are some things I need to take care of. Thanks for the meal, I appreciate it."

"Not a problem. And it was a barter, not a favor, remember?"

He didn't so much as twitch his lips at her small joke.

"Is everything okay?" she asked quietly. "Is Bob okay?"

"He's fine. He got a little wound up about something, and they had to give him a sedative."

She bit her tongue before she could ask more. Clearly, he didn't want to talk about it. And she'd already overstepped.

"I can make your ice cream to go if you'd like."

"Thanks, but I don't want to cut into your stash."

Let it go, Bishop. The man clearly wants to get out of here.

She followed him to the door. They faced each other across the threshold.

He looked tired all of a sudden, the lines around his mouth and eyes more deeply etched. A small frown wrinkled the skin between his eyebrows.

"Thanks for helping with the fuse."

"It was no big deal."

"Those of us who are once again experiencing the joys of electricity beg to differ."

He mustered a small, distracted smile. "I'll see you around."

She stood in the doorway until he'd disappeared next door. Then she went back to the kitchen. The ice cream had gone soft around the edges. She put the lids on and returned both tubs to the freezer.

She went out to the deck and collected their empty bottles, pulling the French doors shut behind herself when she entered the house. She put the dishes in the dishwasher, packed away the leftovers.

And still she felt restless and edgy and itchy and scratchy.

Relax. You'll probably never see him again, Bishop.

Which was a good thing, because instinct told her that Tyler Adamson wasn't the easy-come-easy-go kind of lover she'd been limiting herself to the past few years. In fact, instinct told her that there was nothing easy or forgettable about the man at all.

She considered that moment toward the end of their dinner when she'd made the joke about needing a cigarette and he'd looked into her eyes and she'd known, absolutely, that they were both thinking about things a lot hotter than ice cream.

Definitely it would be a good thing if she never saw him again.

Crossing to the French doors, she called Mr. Whiskers in from the garden. Then she took herself to bed.

CHAPTER THREE

TYLER THREW THE PILLOW on the couch and sat to untie the laces on his work boots. Despite the fact that the windows had been open all day and he'd cleared out all the moldering newspapers, the room still smelled faintly of must and dust.

Awesome.

By rights, he should be halfway to Melbourne by now. Halfway to his own place and his own bed and his own life. Instead, he was preparing to spend the night on the couch in his parents' house.

He could have bunked in his old room, of course. He'd pushed open the door this afternoon and seen that his single bed was still shoved up against the wall in the corner, even though every other trace of his presence had been eradicated, down to the initials he'd carved in the window ledge.

His father would have had to fill and sand and paint the ledge to remove those initials. Several hours work, no small thing.

The house was still warm after the heat of the day and he stripped down to his boxer-briefs and stretched out on the couch. His feet hung over the arm and something hard pressed into his back.

He rolled onto his side. The couch might be uncomfortable, but it was better than being in that little closet of a room, fighting off too many bad memories.

About a million times better.

He closed his eyes, but his mind was full of the phone conversation he'd just had with the nurse on his father's ward.

"Your father has expressed himself quite vehemently, Mr. Adamson," Sister Kemp said. "He wants to go home to die."

Apparently they'd sicced the social worker on his father this afternoon to talk about his plans for the future and at the first mention of a hospice his father had started raising hell and hadn't stopped until they'd fed something into his I.V. to calm him down.

"We'll be having a meeting to discuss his situation tomorrow morning and it would be helpful if a member of the family could be present," Sister Kemp had explained.

It wasn't as though Tyler had had any option except to agree to be there, hence the necessity to stay the night. Like it or not, Robert Adamson was his father. His responsibility. Even if they were as distant as strangers.

The phone call had destroyed the small oasis of pleasure he'd found in the evening. Talking with Ally Bishop, laughing with her, had been the highlight of his day. Hands down.

He thought about the way she'd bristled when he stepped in to fix her fuse box and despite everything—the shitty couch, the knowledge that staying overnight would put him even further behind at work, the fact that he could feel himself getting sucked into a situation he wanted nothing to do with—he smiled. She was a feisty piece of work, that was for sure. Pretty funny, since she barely came up to his armpit and looked about as fierce as a puppy.

She was a smart lady. Straight-up, too. He appreciated the way she'd seized the bull by the horns and apologized to him this afternoon. She'd looked him in the eye and humbled herself with no excuses.

Hard not to admire that.

Or the way she'd diplomatically steered clear of the subject of his father all evening. He didn't know what his father had told her about their relationship—didn't want to know, either—but he appreciated the way she'd given him some breathing room.

Why don't you go ahead and admit how much you appreciated the way she filled out her tank top, too?

It was true. He'd noticed that his father's next-door neighbor had nice breasts. Full, but not too big. A good, firm handful, if he was any judge. He'd also noticed that she had the sort of mouth that was used to smiling and a round, curvy little behind that bounced ever so slightly when she walked.

So, not so much a righteous elf, then. More a sexy,

cute one. With feminist leanings and a love of ice cream.

His smile faded as his thoughts circled to his father again. He'd committed himself to tomorrow's meeting, and he could distract himself all he wanted but it wasn't going to make any difference to the decision that lay ahead.

He rolled onto his back and folded his arms behind his head. It was going to be a long night.

TEN HOURS LATER, TYLER exited the Kyneton District Hospital family meeting room and glanced around to get his bearings. He had a pocketful of paperwork and business cards and what felt like the weight of the world on his shoulders.

Spotting a sign indicating reception was to his right, he started walking. A few minutes later, he stopped outside his father's room.

He'd just listened to two nurses, a doctor and the social worker explain the likely progression of his father's disease. They'd talked about palliative care and the facilities available locally, and they'd talked about the kind of support his father would need if he was to go home to die, as he'd requested.

The reality was, while the government could provide some support for at-home care, they couldn't cover it all. If his father was to go home, Tyler would need to get involved. He'd need to hire a private nurse, sort out his father's cooking-and-cleaning requirements, manage his medical treatment. And if that was a task he wasn't prepared to take on, Robert Adamson would be forced into a hospice against his will.

It would be the ultimate revenge. Walking away and letting his father reap what he had sown—a faceless, nameless death in a state institution, the ideal punishment for a man who had withheld affection and compassion and understanding from his own children. If ever Tyler had wanted to pay back his father for the beatings, the denigration, the lack of interest, the small-mindedness, this was his moment.

Tyler took the final step through his father's doorway. Robert was sleeping and Tyler walked quietly to his side. His father's complexion was pale and his breathing seemed labored. His eyelids flickered as he slept.

Tyler wondered what his father dreamed about, if he dreamed at all. Tyler preferred not to dream, although usually it wasn't a matter of choice. His least-favorite recurring nightmare was the one where his father tortured his and Jon's dog, Astro, to teach Tyler a lesson.

Tyler had been late getting home for dinner, an offense that usually led to a dressing down and a cuff over the ear or a few hits with the belt. But this time his father had simply given him a long, hard look before resuming eating his meal. At first Tyler had been relieved that his father had said nothing. Then he'd been scared.

The next day, his father waited until Tyler was

about to head off to school before backing the car very deliberately over Astro's tail as the dog lay sleeping in a sunny spot beside the driveway.

The dog had yelped with pain, its cries high-pitched and disturbing. His father only rolled the car forward after Tyler had tearfully begged for forgiveness and promised never to be late again.

As usual, there had been precious little sympathy from his mother. "Every action has a consequence," she'd said. "Perhaps now you won't be so quick to be inconsiderate of others."

Tyler had waited a week, then he'd smuggled the dog out of the yard and given him to one of his friends from school. He'd told his parents that he'd left the gate open. He'd been punished for being careless, and Jon had hated him for taking away the one source of love and comfort in their lives, but it was the only way he'd seen to protect his beloved pet.

He'd been eight years old.

Familiar anger and outrage burned in Tyler's gut. As an adult, he could appreciate how masterful his father's choice of punishment had been. What he couldn't understand was the cold calculation that had been behind the act. What kind of man invested time and energy in devising ways to torture his children?

Tyler's hands fisted.

Tell me why I should do this for you, old man. Give me one good reason why I should turn my life upside down so that you can have some peace.

His father stirred in his sleep. The heart monitor kept up its steady rhythm.

Tyler tried to dredge up one good memory. One moment that wasn't infused with fear or disappointment or anger.

A Christmas came to him, hazy, tinted in sepia tones. Wrapping paper everywhere, his mother smiling indulgently for once instead of worrying about keeping everything clean and tidy. There'd been a present, a big one, a combined gift for him and Jon. They'd torn the paper off to find a ride-on wooden train, complete with coal truck and two carriages. The engine had been a shiny cherry-red, the coal truck glossy black, the wheels tricked out in yellow. His father had watched, an expectant light in his eye, soaking up their delight as they ran their hands over their prize and started arguing over who would have the first ride.

"Your father's been putting that together in the shed for the past month," their mother had explained.

Tyler couldn't remember what had happened next. Had they thanked their father? Had they been surprised by such generosity from a man they'd already learned to regard with caution?

He had no idea.

His father stirred again, shifting on the pillow. His face creased with pain and he murmured something beneath his breath. His eyes opened and Tyler met his cloudy gaze.

"I thought you went back to town," his father said.

"The hospital called me last night."

His father's gaze slid over Tyler's shoulder. He was embarrassed, Tyler realized.

"It's my life. Should be my death, too. Anybody would have gotten upset."

"You want to go home."

"They said they wouldn't let me. That they'd get in trouble if they sent me home alone. But I don't need anybody. Been looking after myself for years. Anyway, it's none of their business."

Tyler could hear the desperation in his father's voice. It made his gut tight. Funny, but he'd almost prefer his father yell at him. Seeing him scared like this, beaten… It messed with his vision of the world too much.

"I've got some stuff to sort out in Melbourne, but I'll be back to make arrangements for you. Someone to come in to cook for you and look after the cleaning. And a nurse to manage your medical care. The hospital wants to assess the house, too. Make sure there's good access and that the bathroom's safe for you to use. But if we can cover off the other stuff, they say you're good to go."

"You mean, I can go home? They won't make me stay here?" His father sounded as though he was afraid to hope.

"Yeah, Dad. You can go home."

Tyler waited for him to say something—anything—but he didn't. He simply stared at Tyler for a long moment. Then he blinked and a single tear slid from the corner of his eye and down his cheek onto the pillow.

Tyler looked away.

"The nurses have my number. Call me if you need anything. I'll be back on Monday."

He didn't wait for a reply, simply headed for the door.

There was nothing more to say, after all. He was doing the right thing. Being a dutiful son.

Three cheers for him.

"HERE HE IS. STILL ALIVE and purring. Still shedding on the couch and licking his privates at every opportunity," Ally said.

The large tabby cat in her arms squirmed, trying to escape, but Ally kept him positioned in front of the built-in camera on her laptop. Wendy smiled and waved from inside the frame on the computer screen.

"There's my baby. How you doin', little guy? You missing your mommy? You missing me, buddy?"

Ally cleared her throat. "Um. Do you want me to leave you two alone for a minute…?"

"Shut up. Just because I love my pet."

"You should go the whole hog and have a baby. Stop kidding yourself," Ally said.

"A cat is not a baby substitute," Wendy said.

"You're right. A baby would be less trouble. And he wouldn't leave fur everywhere."

"Says the footloose and fancy-free Ms. Bishop."

The doorbell rang, echoing down the hallway. Ally wheeled the chair back from the desk.

"There's someone at the front door," she said. "It might be the postman with that parcel you're waiting on. Give me a tick to check..."

She left the study, her bare feet padding softly on the wide, worn floorboards. She pulled the door open, expecting to see a blue uniform and a clipboard for her to sign. Instead, she found herself staring at a broad, muscular chest covered in a black cotton T-shirt.

"You're back," she said as she lifted her gaze to Tyler's face.

"It's a long story." He offered her a tight smile, his silver-gray eyes unreadable. "Do you have a minute?"

"I do. At least, I will have. I'm just finishing up a Skype call. But I won't be a sec." She gestured for him to come inside, then hustled down the hallway. She was aware of him shutting the door and following her before she ducked into the study.

"Wendy, gotta go. I'll catch you later, okay?"

"All right, but don't forget to give Mr. Whiskers his flea stuff. And he's due for his worming tablet. You might have to hide it in his dinner to get him to eat it."

"I can handle it, don't worry," Ally said. After three years of wrangling other people's pets, she was an expert at stroking throats and hiding pills in food.

"Speak soon, okay?" she said.

She clicked the mouse to end the call and turned to find Tyler standing in the doorway, a slight frown on his face as he scanned the spines of the many accounting and finance manuals on her friend's bookshelf.

"Sorry about that," she said.

Tyler shifted his attention to her. "You've got a lot of business books for an advice columnist."

She laughed. "They're not mine. God, no. I can barely add two and two. They're Wendy's. I'm house-sitting for her while she's away."

"So this isn't your place?"

"Nope."

His frown deepened.

"Would you like a coffee?" she asked.

"That'd be great, thanks."

She led him into the kitchen and filled the kettle at the sink. She hadn't expected to see him again. Or at least not so soon. She told herself that was why she was feeling a little skittish and self-conscious.

"Did you see Bob this morning? How's he doing?"

"He's good. A little slow to shake off whatever they gave him last night, but otherwise he seemed okay."

"Oh, good. Do you think he'll be up for a visit again this afternoon?" She grabbed two mugs and opened the fridge, searching for the milk.

"Sure."

She studied him over the open fridge door, noting the way he was standing so stiffly. Like a customer in a coffee shop. He'd indicated he wanted to talk, but she had the feeling that she might be waiting all day if she let him work his way around to the purpose of his visit.

She shut the fridge and regarded him frankly.

"Would it help any if I said that whatever it is, I'm happy to help?"

He looked a little taken aback for a moment. Then he rubbed the back of his neck self-consciously. "I'm that obvious, am I?"

"Let's just say you should never play high-stakes poker."

"Thanks for the tip."

"Is it something to do with Bob? Please don't tell me you want me to break it to him that his newspaper collection is gone."

"Dad wants to come home."

She swallowed as the implications inherent in that one small statement hit home.

"I told him I'd arrange things to make it happen, and I can sort out a nurse and someone to handle his meals and things from Melbourne. But the social worker wants to assess the house before she'll agree to discharge him. I've got commitments I can't get out of in town, so..." He pulled a key from the hip pocket of his jeans. "I wondered if you would mind letting her in so she can check the place out and give me her recommendations?"

Ally guessed from the mention of various support staff that Tyler did not plan on nursing his father himself. From what she'd seen of the distance between father and son, she wasn't surprised. In fact, after what she'd seen in the parking lot yesterday, she was surprised Tyler was here at all.

"I can take care of that for you. Not a problem."

"Thanks. I appreciate it."

She held out her hand and he dropped the key into it. The brass was warm from his body and she closed her fingers around it. "Is that all? You don't want to borrow money or ask me to perjure myself on your behalf or bury a body in my backyard?"

It took him a moment to understand she was joking.

"No."

"The way you were looking, I was sure you were about to ask for a vital organ."

"I guess you could say I'm not in the habit of asking favors," he said slowly.

"No kidding. For future reference, I like your father, I'm here during the day and I'm happy to help out in any way I can. Okay?"

He nodded.

"Does that mean you'll ask if there's anything else you or Bob need?"

"Sure," he said, although his posture and the tension in his face told her otherwise.

She shook her head. "Seriously. You should never play cards for money."

His mouth kicked up at the corner. At last. A little more schtick and she might even squeeze a full smile out of him. Why that seemed so important all of a sudden she didn't know, but it did.

"Milk? Sugar?" The kettle was boiling and she poured water into the coffee press.

"Black, thanks."

"Ah, a purist."

"More a pragmatist. The guys at work go through milk like it's going out of fashion, so I figured life would be a lot less disappointing if I got used to having my coffee black."

"That *is* very pragmatic of you. Me, I'd throw a hissy fit until they learned to leave some milk for the boss."

"It's kind of hard for anyone over six foot to pull off a hissy fit. In my experience, anyway."

"True. I hadn't thought of that."

She slid his coffee across the counter toward him. Their fingers brushed briefly as the mug changed hands. She looked up—and got caught in the clear, bright silver of his eyes.

"Has anyone ever told you you have wolf's eyes?" she said before she could stop herself.

He lifted his eyebrows. "Wolf's eyes?"

"The color, I mean," she said, feeling incredibly transparent. "Obviously they're not really hairy or anything."

He took a sip of his coffee. "Can't say that I've heard that before, no."

"Well, now you know."

"Yeah."

His gaze dropped from her face to her chest, then her hips, taking in her Penelope Pitstop pajama pants and matching pink tank top.

"What happened to the cowboys and Indians?"

"Oh, they're after-five wear only. I like to go a little more low-key during the day."

"Ah."

She looked at him over the rim of her mug and her eyes met his and suddenly it was last night all over again, the room crackling with tension and potential. Except this time he wasn't here by accident, and she knew she would definitely be seeing him again.

"Cookies. We need cookies." She crossed to the cupboard, making a big deal out of opening a package of cookies. She didn't quite meet his eyes when she slid the container across the counter toward him.

"I'm good, thanks."

She picked up the tea towel and wiped the counter.

It was just a look, Bishop. Get over it. Hot men have looked at you before. You'll survive.

But none of them had been as…compelling as Tyler.

"Any idea when the hospital people might want to come by?" she asked.

They talked about the appointment and exchanged phone numbers, then Tyler checked his watch and put down his mug.

"I need to go. I've got a client meeting I have to make this afternoon."

She followed him to the front door.

"I should be here again by Monday at the latest," he said.

"Okay. Like I said, call me if you need anything."

He raised his hand in farewell. She told herself to go inside but she remained in the doorway, watching his broad shoulders and firm, round backside as he walked away. He glanced over his shoulder as he passed through the gate, catching her watching him.

Again, their gazes locked and held for a long, sticky beat. Then he kept walking.

Okay, that's going to be a problem.

Last night, the attraction she'd felt for Tyler had been a slightly titillating surprise—a diversion from the mundanity of life, an unexpected blip on her radar. They'd been ships passing in the night, the frisson between them a possibility that had come to nothing. Today...

Today the attraction between them seemed more complicated than titillating.

What's the problem? Nothing is going to happen if you don't want it to.

She knew it was true. And yet, somehow, it wasn't as comforting a thought as it should be.

TYLER ARRIVED AT THE workshop in time to make his client meeting. Afterward, he went straight to his office and checked his schedule for the following week. His diary was full—client meetings, a marketing seminar, a catch-up with one of his major lumber suppliers. For the life of him he didn't see how he could free up enough time to sort out his father's situation. He had an elbow on his desk, his fingers kneading his forehead when Gabby rapped on the door and entered.

"You forgot these," she said, holding up the rolled blueprints from their meeting.

"Thanks," he said. "You were great in the meeting, too, by the way."

She shrugged. "You'd be surprised how much I've picked up being around you guys. I think I could practically make a table myself now."

She turned to leave. Tyler looked at the schedule he'd massacred with red pen and pencil strikes and arrows. He'd been trying to find a way to free up some time, hadn't he?

"Gabby. Before you go."

She gave him an inquiring look.

"How would you feel about taking on more client meetings? Stepping into sales more?"

She looked surprised. "What's brought this on?"

"I need some time off. At least from the day-to-day stuff. I can take the briefs with me, keep working on the designs, but I can't keep driving back and forth all the time."

Gabby frowned, confused. "Sorry?"

Tyler realized he'd skipped an important beat.

"My father wants to be home to die. I told him I'd organize things so that could happen, but I need to be in Woodend to do that in the short-term—"

"Oh, Tyler. That's so sad. I didn't realize things were that serious. Are you okay?"

He shrugged. "Of course."

"There's no *of course* about it. He's your father."

Tyler made a pointless mark on the page in front of him. "In name only."

Gabby shook her head. "You drive me crazy, you know that?"

She rounded the desk and put her arms around him, resting her cheek against his. For a moment he was enveloped in her scent, still familiar despite the fact that it had been two years since they'd been lovers.

His thoughts shifted to Ally. He'd caught a trace of her scent when she'd brushed past him this morning. Vanilla and spice. Completely different from Gabby's lemon freshness.

This wasn't the first time his thoughts had drifted to his father's next-door neighbor today. He'd thought about her on and off during the drive to Melbourne. The way her eyes lit when she laughed. The round fullness of her breasts. The look they'd shared when he'd glanced over his shoulder as he was leaving and caught her watching him.

"It's not a crime to accept a little comfort, Tyler," Gabby said as she stepped back from him.

"I don't need comfort. I need time. Do you think you can do it or not?"

"I might have to juggle some of the admin stuff, but I don't see why not. How many weeks do you need?"

"I only need a few days."

Gabby looked stricken. "He's that bad?"

"They don't know. It could be weeks, it could be months."

"Then maybe we should think more long-term than a week so—"

"I'm getting him a nurse. I just need some time to get things organized, that's all." How many times did he have to say this to people?

"You're not staying with him yourself?" He could hear the censure in her tone.

"No."

Gabby looked as though she wanted to say more, but after a long moment she simply nodded, her lips thin. "It's your life, Tyler. Tell me what you need me to do and I'll do it."

"Thanks. I'll draw up a list of appointments for you."

She nodded, then exited his office.

He knew what she was thinking—that he was cold because he planned on hiring people to nurse his father in his final days.

Maybe he *was* cold. Why not? He'd been taught by a master. Why should he know the first thing about being kind when all he'd been fed as a child was intolerance, impatience and rage?

For the first time it occurred to him that there had been no judgment in Ally's face or voice when he'd told her his plans this morning. She'd simply heard him out and offered her help.

She was an interesting woman. Generous, too—he'd been surprised when he'd learned she'd been living beside his father for only a few weeks. She'd been so fired up on his father's behalf, he'd simply assumed their relationship was one of long standing.

He frowned as he registered what he was doing—thinking about his father's neighbor again.

He couldn't decide if it was a good thing or a bad thing. Obviously he was attracted to her. But he wasn't exactly in a position to get involved with anyone or anything right now. Thanks to his father, his cup was about to runneth over.

Which probably meant he should stop thinking about her. And that he should keep his distance when he returned to Woodend.

He returned his attention to his diary. Reality check—he didn't have the time to be thinking about a woman. Even one as interesting and attractive as Ally Bishop.

CHAPTER FOUR

THE SOCIAL WORKER CAME the following day. Ally showed the woman around Bob's house, took note of her recommendations, then made a couple of quick phone calls before pulling Tyler's business card from where she'd stuck it behind a magnet on the fridge door.

She ran her fingertips over the embossed lettering on the card, thinking about his silver-gray eyes and broad shoulders, then she punched his number into her phone.

"Tyler speaking."

His voice sounded incredibly deep and low over the phone.

"It's me, Ally. The social worker's just been."

"That was quick."

"She said she didn't want to hold things up at her end."

A weary sigh came down the line. "Which means Dad's probably been throwing his weight around again."

"He seemed okay when I saw him this morning. I think he understands he can't go home until the doctors are happy with his recovery from the surgery, so he's been making an effort to eat more and he's been paying attention to his physiotherapist."

"Listen, thanks, Ally. I appreciate you helping out like this."

Ally glanced down at the notes she'd taken. "I've got a list of her recommendations, if you want to hear them?"

"Sure. Thanks."

"She's suggested safety rails at both the front and rear steps as well as in the shower. And she would like to see a handheld showerhead in the bathroom and a bath chair for your father to sit on if he's feeling weak."

"Okay." He sounded as though he was making notes. "Anything else?"

"She said the bedroom doorways were wide enough to allow them to install a hospital bed, if one is required at a later date, but that Bob's own bed would be fine for now."

"That's good to know."

"I wasn't sure if you wanted to do the work yourself, being handy and everything, but she's recommended a local guy and I took the liberty of making a quick call. He can take care of everything on Friday, if you want him to, or the following Monday."

There was a short pause. "Friday, you said?"

"Yeah. He said he could fit you in in the afternoon. If it's a problem for you to get here, I can let him into the house, since I've still got your spare key. It's no big deal."

There was another short silence. "That's very generous of you."

"It really isn't. It'll take two seconds to let him in. And you've got enough on your plate."

She waited for him to tell her to butt out. Or to ask why she kept inserting herself into his and Bob's lives. Usually she confined her do-gooding to her advice column, but for some reason she couldn't seem to stop herself where Bob and Tyler were concerned.

"I read your column today," Tyler said instead.

It was so not what she'd expected him to say that it took her a moment to respond. "Did you?"

"Yeah. The bit about the guy who dresses as a woman."

"Right."

"Turns out that all my staff read you, too."

"That's nice. I think. What did they say about the cross-dressing guy?" She could imagine the comments that must have been flying around. Especially in a very macho environment like a workshop.

"Turns out my senior cabinetmaker has a cousin who works as a drag queen."

"Well, there you go."

"You must get some pretty weird letters."

"I get some very weird letters. But underneath the weirdness, it's amazing how much the same we all are."

"How so?" Tyler asked.

"Everyone wants to be accepted. Everyone wants

to belong. Everyone wants to love and be loved. To feel valued."

"Is that what you want?"

Ally thought about the way she'd taken it upon herself to call the handyman today, and the way she'd thrust herself into Bob's affairs. "I think everyone wants to feel connected, in some small way," she said quietly.

"I guess."

She heard the rustle of paper at the other end of the phone, as though he was shifting things around on his desk.

"So, do you want me to let this guy in?" she asked.

"If you don't mind. It'd be one less thing on my list. We're snowed under at the moment—"

"Then don't think about it again. I'll get the guy to bill you at your factory address, okay?"

"That'd be great."

She told herself to hang up before the conversation strayed any further than it already had.

"You still think you'll be here on Monday?" She winced. Could she sound more obvious and hopeful?

"I'm planning for Sunday at this point. The hospital said Dad might be able to come home Monday, so I wanted to get some food in, that kind of thing."

"I guess I'll see you then, then."

"You will."

There was something in the way he said it that

made her sit holding the phone for a good sixty seconds after she'd ended the call.

It had almost sounded like a promise.

TYLER PULLED UP IN FRONT of his father's house at dusk on Sunday night. He'd spent the past few days working late at the workshop, clearing his desk as much as possible, covering things off with Gabby to ensure she had all she needed to take over his client meetings.

Ally had called him once more to let him know the safety rails and new bathroom fittings had been installed. He'd never been big on talking on the phone, but he'd caught himself attempting to stretch their conversation into more than an update on his father's house remodeling. She'd answered his questions and teased him and asked some of her own, then she'd suddenly clammed up and the conversation had ended.

He glanced at her place as he grabbed his bags from the bed of the truck. Maybe he was misreading things. For all he knew, she could have a boyfriend. Maybe that was why she'd suddenly backed off. He knew nothing about her or her situation—all he had to go on was his gut and those few loaded moments when he'd been intensely aware of her as a woman. But maybe that was all one-sided.

And maybe he was simply looking for something—anything—to distract himself from the grim reality of his situation. Over the past few days he'd become aware of a reluctance within himself to think beyond the nuts and bolts of arranging for his father's respite care. Nurses and social workers he could handle, but the prospect of standing by his father's graveside left him unsettled and uneasy. Not because he cared. He refused to care—although he couldn't explain his reluctance to acknowledge his father's mortality in any other way.

He dumped all but one of his burdens on the front porch of his father's house before making his way next door. Ally still had the spare key, and he had a gift to thank her for her help with the house.

Plus he wanted to see her, distraction or not.

The hall light was on inside the house and the stained-glass panels of the door glowed with rich color as he raised his hand to knock. He saw a shadow approach, then the door opened and she was standing there, cuter and fresher and sexier than he'd remembered. His gaze automatically dropped below her waist and he didn't try to hide the smile tugging at his mouth as he saw today's pajama pants.

"Scooby-Doo. Nice choice," he said.

"I thought so," she said. "Not too dressy, not too informal. A smart-casual kind of a pajama pant."

He held up the small ice chest in his hand. "For you."

Her eyebrows rose as she reached out to take the chest. "For me?"

"To say thank-you."

"For letting a couple of people in next door?" Her

expression told him she considered it the smallest of favors.

"For giving a shit when you didn't have to. If you'll excuse my French. You barely know my father, yet you've bent over backward for him. Not many people put themselves out like that anymore."

"You make me want to find a mirror to check my halo's on straight."

But her cheeks were pink and he could see that she was pleased.

He gestured toward the cooler. "You might want to get that in the freezer."

There was plenty of ice in the chest, but the sooner the contents were below zero the better.

She cracked the lid on the chest. "You bought me ice cream?"

"Dairy Bell Nuts About Chocolate. You mentioned you like it."

"I do. I love it." She seemed thrown. As though no one had ever bought her ice cream before. "You should come in."

"I don't want to get in your hair. I just wanted to pick up the key."

"You mean, you don't want any of this ice cream?" A smile curled the corner of her mouth.

"I do. But I don't want to outstay my welcome."

"As long as you don't hog the lion's share, you're safe."

She gestured for him to follow her into the kitchen.

"You know, I was just wondering what to have for dinner," she said.

"You mean, dessert."

She gave him a cheeky look. "I mean, dinner."

He laughed.

"Big bowl or little bowl?" she asked.

"What kind of question is that?"

"Big bowl it is, then."

She served up two generous portions then led him out onto the side deck.

"This is my favorite ice cream eating spot." She walked to the three stairs leading into the garden and sat on the top step, shooting a glance up at him.

The outside light cast a golden sheen over her hair and face. He looked at her for a long beat, trying to understand why he found her so appealing. She was cute, yes, but not beautiful. And her baggy pajama pants should have been an antidote to sexual desire. But all he could think about were the curves hidden beneath the bright fabric.

"You want to sit at the table?" she asked, starting to rise.

"Here is fine."

He sat beside her, forcing himself to gaze out at the dark garden rather than watch as she licked her spoon.

"Your friend has a nice place here. Good garden."

"Tell me about it. I'm living in fear that I'll kill

everything with my black thumb before she gets back."

He swallowed a mouthful of creamy chocolate and pecans. "So where do you hang out when you're not house-sitting?"

"I'm always house-sitting."

He raised an eyebrow and she shrugged a shoulder.

"I do this on a semiprofessional basis. There are a bunch of house-sitting websites out there, and I look around for jobs that suit me, then apply to look after peoples' homes for them while they're away. I get free room and board, they get to know their pets and gardens and valuables are being looked after."

He paused with his spoon halfway to his mouth, processing what she'd said.

"So you don't have a place of your own, a base?"

"Nope." She closed her eyes as she ate another mouthful. "God, I love the way they mix that chocolate fudge stuff all through it. I wonder what they put in it to keep it all gooey like that?"

Tyler was still trying to get his head around what she'd told him. "What about your stuff? You must have a storage locker somewhere."

"Nope."

"What about your mail?"

"The *Herald* forwards it to me with the Dear Gertrude letters." She laughed. "You should see your face. Nesters always freak out when I tell them I live out of a suitcase."

Tyler frowned. "I'm not a nester."

She smiled mysteriously.

"I'm not. Guys don't nest," he said.

"Do you own your own home?"

"Yes."

"Thought so. It's an old one, too, isn't it?"

"Early Victorian."

"And I bet you've renovated it. Stripped back the floors, restored the fireplaces…?"

She had to be guessing, but it was uncanny how close to the mark she was.

She pointed her spoon at him. "You're a nester. Nothing to be ashamed of. I, on the other hand, am not. Can't stand to be pinned down. Hate staying in one spot for too long. Don't see the point of owning a bunch of stuff. Well, except for pajama pants, but they pack light."

"You must have had a place of your own at some point."

"Sure. Before I decided to stop fighting genetics."

"There's a gene for nomadism?"

"Might as well be. My mother was an artist. I spent my childhood either traveling with her or living with my aunt Phyllis or my grandmother. My mom was a gypsy, and so am I, and it's much easier to go with the flow than fight against it. Believe me." Her gaze grew distant, as though she was remembering something hard or painful.

He studied her profile, wondering. The lifestyle she described sounded free and easy—and lonely. He couldn't imagine not having a place to come home to. A sanctuary that was all his. A circle of friends who knew him intimately, who understood his history and his moods and his sense of humor. As a furniture designer, he had a strong appreciation of history and place. Every time he put pen to paper or chisel to wood, he aimed to create family heirlooms, pieces that would be well-loved and well-used. One of the most satisfying aspects of his work was the idea that his furniture became an integral part of his customers' lives and homes.

But Ally had no home. No place to call her own. No sanctuary. No treasured window seat or favorite corner of the garden or sentimental piece of crockery or glassware.

"And you're never tempted to stop and stay?"

She chased a pecan around her bowl for a few beats before replying. "A few times. But you can't fight nature, and it usually means I end up letting someone down. That's why I do the house-sitting thing now. It suits me, and I suit it, and the rest takes care of itself."

"So when your friend comes back, whenever that is, you'll just pack up your duffel and hit the road again?"

"Absolutely. When Wendy finishes her training course in another six weeks' time, I'll pack up my suitcase and go to Sydney, or maybe Brisbane. I haven't decided yet."

She inspected her empty bowl, scraping the spoon

against the surface to capture the last traces of ice cream. "It would be wrong to have a second serving, wouldn't it? An invitation to Type 2 diabetes," she said wistfully.

"Sometimes it pays to live dangerously."

"Says the man with the six-pack abs."

She blushed as soon as she said it. He felt a smile tug at his mouth. Nice to have the reassurance that she was as aware of him as he was of her.

"I don't have a six-pack."

"Okay, a four-pack. And if I go back for seconds, it won't be long before I have a keg."

She fussed around, stacking the bowls. Then she shot him a quick look from beneath her lashes. He didn't bother trying to hide his grin. Her expression became rueful.

"No need to look so pleased with yourself."

"I'm not. You just answered a question I've been asking myself, that's all."

A crease appeared between her eyebrows. "What question?"

"This one." He leaned across the space that separated them and pressed his mouth to hers.

Her lips were warm and soft and they opened on a surprised inhalation as he kissed her. He waited, keeping the kiss light, even though he'd been wanting to taste her for a long time. After a torturous beat, her mouth moved beneath his and she returned the pressure of his kiss. He palmed the nape of her neck and slid his tongue into her mouth.

She tasted like chocolate, hot and dark and mysterious. Her tongue slid along his, tentatively at first, then with more confidence. He angled his body toward her, leaning closer, wanting more. She gave an encouraging little moan, her hands sliding to his shoulders.

Heat fired in his belly as he felt the weight of her breasts against his chest and inhaled her scent. Vanilla and cloves, sweet and exotic. Their tongues slid and teased, her hunger matching his.

He hadn't been with a woman for months. And he'd been thinking about Ally all week. Wondering. Fantasizing.

He slid his hand from the nape of her neck, down her arm and onto her rib cage, just beneath the swell of her breasts. He was as hard as a rock, his breath coming fast even though they'd barely started. She clenched her hands in his T-shirt and pulled him even closer, her mouth avid on his.

She was so hot, so sexy, so warm and giving. He slid his hand onto her breast, reveling in the warm, resilient weight of her in his palm, his thumb sweeping across the curve in search of her nipple. She was already hard, the peak straining for his attention and he ran his thumb back and forth over it, smiling against her lips as he felt her shudder in response. He squeezed her nipple between thumb and forefinger and she moaned again and pressed herself into his hand.

He'd known it would be like this between them.

Ever since that moment over their impromptu dinner when she'd made a joke about needing a cigarette after their ice cream discussion. She was earthy and human and real, and he wanted her beneath him, wanted to slide his hands inside her ridiculous, sex-less cartoon pajama pants and discover the warm curves of her hips and backside and thighs.

But first he wanted to taste her breasts. Wrapping his arms around her, he hauled her into his lap. He wanted to make her shudder some more, wanted to explore the soft, scented skin of her neck and breasts and belly, wanted to tease her with his mouth and his tongue and his teeth until neither of them could take it a moment longer.

He moved his hand to the hem of her tank top and lifted it, sliding his hand onto the warm skin of her belly as he kissed her deeply. He slid his hand higher, up her rib cage, already imagining the silk of her breasts against his hands, the way her—

"Wait."

She said the word against his mouth as he was about to cup her breast. He stilled, even though he was hard and desperate to be inside her.

She pulled away from him. He let his hand slide down her rib cage to rest on her hip. She felt so good. So warm and soft and alive.

"This is a bad idea." It would have sounded a hell of a lot more convincing if she hadn't been breathing as heavily as he was.

"Why?" He felt like a teenager voicing the

question. It had been a long time since a woman said no to him.

"Because it won't work."

She slid from his lap, and even though it had been a hot day and a warm night, he felt the loss of her body heat.

"Unless things have changed drastically since I last did this, I think we were doing okay."

She straightened her tank top, then took a deep breath. "I'm leaving in six weeks. And your father is dying."

"I'm not sure what either of those things has to do with us having sex." He could hear the frustration in his own voice.

"Let me ask you this, then. When was the last time you had a one-night stand?"

He raised his eyebrows, a little taken aback by her question. "I can't remember."

"Exactly." She stood and dusted off the seat of her pajama pants.

He stared up at her, affronted. "So, what, because I usually like to know more than a woman's name before I sleep with her you're kicking me to the curb?"

"I'm kicking you to the curb because I like you, Tyler Adamson. Us getting involved would be a mistake. You're the kind of man who wants more than sex and a few laughs, and I'm the kind of girl who leaves."

"You're making a lot of assumptions."

She gave him a level, knowing, very adult look. Then she reached out and took his hand, pressing her fingers to the pulse point at his wrist. He knew what she could feel there—his heart, still pounding away like a tom-tom, demanding more, wanting more. Wordless, she reversed their grips, pressing her own wrist against his fingertips. He felt an answering rhythm beating through her body, just as wild, just as demanding.

"I don't know about you, but that doesn't happen for me every day," she said quietly.

"All the more reason to do something about it."

He told himself to stop before he begged or reduced himself to the old blue-balls gambit, but everything in him resisted the way she was closing the door on the possibilities between them.

He liked her. He wanted to get to know her. Since when had that been a deal-breaker when it came to sex?

"I'm doing you a favor." There was finality in her voice. And regardless of the frustration he felt, he wasn't about to try to importune her into bed.

"Your call," he said, standing.

They were both silent as they walked to the door.

She handed him the spare key on the threshold. "Thanks for the ice cream."

"Like I said, I appreciate your time." He sounded stiff, formal. Pissed off.

Because he hadn't gotten his way? He didn't like

the idea that he was so petty. That his goodwill toward her depended on her bowing to his sexual will. He liked a hell of a lot more about her than her body.

He tried again.

"Thanks for sharing it with me."

"It seemed only fair."

His gaze slid to her mouth. Her bottom lip was slightly swollen, very pink. He remembered the soft, warm press of it against his.

If she hadn't called a halt, he'd be inside her right now, driving them both a little bit crazy.

"Good night, Ally."

"Good night, Tyler."

He heard the door close behind him. His bags were where he'd left them on the porch and he let himself in then dumped them beside the couch in the living room.

The house wasn't as musty as he'd remembered, and he saw that someone had left a vase of wildflowers on the mantle and that one of the windows was open a few inches, letting in the fresh night air.

Ally, of course.

He walked to the bathroom to inspect the safety rails that had been installed. He'd been so eager to see her that he hadn't paused to inspect the set beside the front steps.

A waterproof chair was in the shower stall, ready for his father's return, and a handheld showerhead was fitted alongside the regular one. The safety rails were good-quality chrome, their surface cross-hatched for grip. He noted with approval that the installer had fixed them into the stud instead of relying on plaster fasteners. Over all, a good job. He made a mental note to send a thank-you email to the contractor.

He returned to the living room, feeling restless, and yes, frustrated.

He'd driven to Woodend this evening with an idea in his mind about the way the immediate future might pan out. Useless to pretend that Ally hadn't featured prominently. He'd anticipated getting to know her. He'd hoped to sleep with her, to act on the tension and attraction that crackled between them every time they met. He hadn't gone much beyond that in his mind, but there'd been a sense of potential around his feelings for her.

But Ally wasn't interested. What had she said again? *I like you. Us getting involved would be a mistake.* Then she'd held his fingers to her pulse so he understood that she was as aroused and fired up as he was.

Yet she'd turned him away. Because—and he still couldn't quite get his head around it—he couldn't remember the last time he'd had a one-night stand.

What did that mean? That she only slept with "slam, bam, thank you, ma'am," kind of guys? That she wasn't interested in liking or getting to know the person she was naked with?

He collected his toothbrush and toothpaste from his bag. He thought about the other thing Ally had said as he returned to the bathroom to brush his teeth.

I don't know about you, but that doesn't happen for me every day.

It hadn't happened that way for him for years. Not since he'd been a teenager, wild and horny and needy. One touch of her, one taste and he'd been on fire, game for anything. The odds were good that if she hadn't called a halt he'd have gotten her naked right there on the deck, he'd been so carried away.

And now he was hard all over again, simply from thinking about her.

Better get over that quickly, mate, because it's not going to happen.

He was disappointed. More so than the situation probably warranted. Rationally, the world wasn't going to end tomorrow because a woman he'd met a few times didn't want to explore the attraction between them. Life was full of small missed opportunities.

Suck it up, big guy.

He spat toothpaste into the basin, rinsed his mouth and dried his face. Then he took himself back to the couch and another bad night's sleep.

AFTER TOSSING AND TURNING for nearly two hours, Ally got out of bed and had a cold shower. Embarrassing to admit to herself how unsettled and aroused she was after a few hot and heavy moments in Tyler's arms. They'd pressed against each other and kissed for no more than five minutes, ten tops—and hours later her body was still humming with need.

This is why he's dangerous. You're always attracted to men you can't have.

She let the cold water hammer the back of her neck, the place where she could still feel the imprint of Tyler's hand against her skin.

The way he'd kissed her...

The extraordinary thrill of need and desire that had rippled through her when he'd slid his hand onto her breast...

In that small breathless moment her imagination had rampaged ahead. She'd seen Tyler peeling off her clothes. Seen herself stripping him of his. She'd imagined him on top of her, big and strong, her legs around his hips. The welcome, masculine weight of him pressing her down. Then, the push of him as he slid inside her, filling her...

She'd wanted it all so badly. Too badly. Too much. An alarm had sounded in the back of her mind, a warning that this was too intense, that he was too much. That if they took this to the inevitable conclusion, it would be much more than a quick roll in the hay with the sexy guy from next door.

Ten years ago, when she'd been in her early twenties, Ally would have thrown caution to the wind and dived headfirst into whatever developed between her and Tyler. Sex, or more than sex, or something in between—her younger self would have been up for anything and everything, heedless of the consequences.

She'd prided herself on being a bohemian like her wild, freewheeling artist mother, on being open to experience. And yet it was experience—bitter, sad, shameful experience—that had taught her that some things were not for her.

Daniel had been broken when she'd left him. He'd dreamed of a future for the two of them, and she'd let him. And then, as always, she'd started to feel suffocated and smothered and she'd chipped away at their happiness until Daniel had finally told her to go if she wanted to. And, God help her, she had.

Daniel hadn't been the first man she'd walked away from, but she'd promised herself he would be the last. Unlike her mother, she wasn't willing to toy with other people's emotions in exchange for temporary happiness. And if that meant she was destined to be essentially alone, then so be it.

For the past five years, she'd done her damnedest to stay away from men who made her feel and think and want too much. Men who had the potential to become important in her life. Men, like Tyler, who she sensed she could care for, and who might come to care for her. Men she could hurt and disappoint when she inevitably packed her bags and left. As she always, always did.

She'd had two lovers in those five years, both of them younger than her, both fellow nomads. Good, safe choices, lovers who had offered her the comfort of human contact for a few weeks without the risk of strings.

Not very emotionally satisfying, perhaps. Some might even say empty. But it was better than letting people down.

She turned off the water and stepped onto the bath mat. For a moment she simply stood in the quiet darkness, letting the water roll down her body.

Absurd, but standing here like this, the memory of what had almost happened tonight still resonating within her, she felt an echo of the panic that had dogged her in the last days of her relationship with Daniel.

The need to go. To put him and the mess she'd made of them behind her.

She took a deep breath, then another. She needed to rein herself in. Get a grip—and some much-needed perspective.

She'd kissed Tyler. Pressed herself against him. Fantasized about doing more. And then she'd called a halt.

They'd had four encounters altogether—five, if she counted the time in front of the hospital when she'd seen him break down in his truck. That was it, the sum total of their interactions to date.

So what if the man had brought her ice cream all the way from Melbourne? In an ice chest no less? So what if she found him magnetic and compelling in the extreme? There was absolutely no reason for her to be carrying on like an overwrought and histrionic damsel in distress.

Nothing had happened. Nothing was going to

happen. She'd made that clear, and she knew Tyler had heard her.

She combed her fingers through her hair, scattering droplets. Then she grabbed a towel and blotted away the last of the water from her arms and breasts and belly and legs.

Naked, she walked through the silent house and back to bed.

CHAPTER FIVE

HIS FATHER WAS SITTING on the edge of the bed when Tyler arrived at the hospital the following morning. He was dressed in a wrinkled white shirt and a pair of track pants, and his good black leather loafers sat beside the bed. His hair had been combed flat across his head. A small overnight bag was at the ready on the visitor's chair.

"You're on time," his father said.

"I said I'd be here."

Tyler had been calling the hospital every other day during the week to stay informed on his father's progress, but he hadn't once spoken to his father, and his father had made no effort to contact him.

No surprises there.

Now, they eyed each other silently before his father dipped his head in a small, grudging nod.

Tyler glanced at the overnight bag. "Is this yours?"

"Who else would it belong to?"

Tyler ignored the goad and hefted the bag. "Do we need to sign you out or anything?"

"The head nurse, the gray-haired one, said she had some instructions for you."

"Right."

He left the bag on the bed and exited the room. Sister Kemp was working at the computer when he approached the nurses' station.

"Mr. Adamson," she said as he approached. "You're here bright and early."

"My father is pretty keen to get home. He said you had some instructions for me."

"Yes. The doctor wanted us to be sure to go over your father's medication with you."

They spent the next few minutes reviewing his father's medication, then she handed him some information sheets and a list of numbers.

"If you have any questions or feel out of your depth, call."

"Thanks, Sister."

"It's Carrie. And I mean it about calling. It can be a daunting business, taking care of a loved one."

He didn't bother explaining that he'd hired a nurse for the task. "Thanks for looking after him," he said instead.

"It was a pleasure," Carrie said. "He's a gruff old character, but once you get him chatting he's got a lovely sense of humor. He's had us all in stitches more than once."

"Yeah, he's a real old charmer."

It had always been that way. The teachers at school, his friends' parents, they'd all thought his father was an affable, easygoing guy. When he wanted to, his father knew how to lay on the charm.

He'd simply never bothered to expend any of it on his sons.

Tyler walked back to his father's room.

"Let's go," he said, as he collected the bag.

His father shifted to the edge of the bed, wincing a little. Tyler watched as his father slid his right foot into the loafer, only to frown impatiently as his heel got caught on the back of the shoe. He tried again, but succeeded only in depressing the leather beneath his heel.

"Stupid bloody thing," his father muttered. Then he stuffed his left foot into the other shoe until he'd achieved the same half-assed result and slowly stood.

"You can't walk out like that. You'll trip," Tyler said.

"I'm fine." His father took a couple of shuffling steps to prove his point.

Tyler put down the overnight bag and dropped to one knee in front of his father. "Lift your foot."

"I said I'm fine."

"Do you want to go home or not?"

"You know I do."

"Then lift your foot so I can fix your shoes and we can walk out of here safely."

Probably there were better ways to handle the situation, kinder things to say. His father's pride was clearly stinging at the idea of appearing so helpless in front of the son he once dwarfed. But Tyler wasn't about to pander to him. Not now, not ever. It was enough that he was here. More than enough.

His father muttered under his breath, but he lifted his left foot out of the shoe. Tyler unfolded the leather, then held the shoe at the correct angle to allow his father's foot to slide inside. He repeated the move with the second shoe.

Despite his irritation, it was impossible not to be aware of how profoundly the small act reflected the reversal of their roles.

He pushed himself upright, avoiding his father's eyes. "Let's go."

He knew from his consultations with the nursing staff that his father had been walking the corridors each day in a bid to recover his strength, but his father's steps were still slow. Tyler hovered at his side, one hand at the ready in case his father faltered. When they reached the entrance, he turned to his father.

"Wait here. I'll go grab the truck."

"I can walk."

"Wait here," Tyler repeated.

It wasn't until he was unlocking the door that he noticed his father had ignored him and was slowly shuffling his way across the parking lot.

Stubborn old bastard.

Tyler had a premonition of how the next few days were going to pan out—his father belligerently trying to do everything as though he hadn't had major surgery and a life-changing diagnosis, Tyler playing umpire and trying to curtail his excesses.

Fun and games, to be sure.

By way of rounding off the experience, his father attempted to get into the truck on his own when Tyler pulled up alongside him, ignoring Tyler's order to wait for assistance. By the time they were on the road, Tyler was grinding his teeth with frustration.

"I've arranged for a nurse to visit you twice a day, starting tomorrow," he explained as they drove into town. "She'll check your wound and your medication and help you shower. And there's a meal service I've organized to bring you your meals."

"Don't need a meal service. I can still cook. I'm not dead yet."

"You can't live on canned food."

"What do you think I've been living on?"

Tyler bit his tongue on the observation that his father's current situation was hardly an advertisement for his dietary choices.

"Canned food is full of sodium and additives. The stuff I've arranged for you is fresh."

His father set his jaw. In the old days, it would have meant a flare-up was in the offing, and Tyler and Jon would have made themselves scarce in the hope of avoiding the inevitable fallout. Today, his father merely crossed his arms over his chest and sulked.

When they pulled up in front of the house, his father peered through the windshield, frowning as *he spotted the shiny new handrails on either side of* the steps.

"Where did those ugly things come from?"

"The hospital wanted them installed before they'd let you come home."

"Nobody asked me."

Tyler threw his hands in the air. "Fine. I'll rip the handrails out and you can go into the hospice."

He was so exasperated, he actually started the truck again, ready to follow through on his threat. He knew he was overreacting, that it was stupid to let himself get fired up by his father's pointless objections, but this was new territory for him, too, and he was acutely aware of the contradictory emotions shoving and tugging at him every second he spent in his father's presence. Pity, anger, guilt. And, as much as he hated to admit it, the echo of old fear.

Perhaps that was why he responded so easily to his father's small acts of defiance—deep inside, there was a part of him that still flinched when he saw those expressions of anger and impatience in his father's face.

Some lessons were impossible to unlearn.

"You Adamson blokes don't muck about, do you? I didn't think you'd be home until the afternoon."

It was Ally, standing on the pavement, smiling through the open window.

His father made a disgruntled sound. "Did you see what they've done to my place? Put a bunch of ugly metal all over it. Looks like an old people's home."

Ally pulled a comically concerned face. "Oh, dear. If you don't like those I don't want to be around when you see what they've done to the bathroom."

"The bathroom?" his father said.

"Oh, yes. Safety rails up the kazoo. A veritable forest of shiny chrome. You'll need sunglasses every time you go in there."

His father frowned. Tyler waited for the outburst—the angry words, the insults, the quickly raised fist. Instead, his father's mouth quirked up at the side. Then he gave a little chuckle.

"Is it that bad?" his father asked.

"Worse. And here's the best bit—it's partly my fault because I let the guy in and told him what to do." Ally made another comic face, as though she was bracing herself for the condemnation about to rain down on her.

His father chuckled again. "You're a bloody cheeky thing. Come on, help an old man out."

Tyler watched as his father let Ally support him as he slid from the pickup. It was the first time he'd seen them together and he noted the soft light in her eyes as she looked at his father, the gentle way she held his arm.

He transferred his gaze to his parent, trying to imagine what she must see when she looked at him. But it was impossible for him to remove the filter of his own experiences from his perception. He might be older, frailer, but the man making his way up the sidewalk was still the same man who had filled Tyler's childhood with fear and emptied it of certainty.

He got out and grabbed his father's bag from the truck bed.

Ally and his father were standing at the bottom of the steps when he joined them. His father stared at one of the rails for a long beat, then reached out and rested his hand on it.

"Might as well use the bloomin' things, I suppose. Since you've wasted my money on them."

Tyler bit back on the correction that rose to his lips. He'd wasted his own money making the house safe, not his father's. But this wasn't about money.

His father climbed the steps slowly, then waited while Tyler unlocked the house.

"Why don't I leave you to settle in and come back later for a cup of tea and some cake?" Ally said.

She hovered at the top of the porch steps, ready to descend.

"No, no, come in now. Tyler can make us something," his father insisted.

"Sure. I'll whip up a batch of scones, maybe a pavlova or two."

"I have some cake at my place. Why don't I grab that?" Ally suggested.

For the first time that day Tyler looked at her directly. She was wearing a knee length white skirt with red flowers printed on it and a white tank top. She looked tanned and bright and summery. Her eyes were cautiously warm as they met his. As though she wasn't sure of her reception, but was pleased to see him, anyway.

Had he been that much of a bear last night?

"That'd be great, thanks, Ally," he said.

She gave him a small smile. "I'll be back in two shakes of a lamb's tail."

As she walked away, he traced the shape of her hips and backside with his eyes before returning his attention to getting his father inside the house. He needed to stop noticing how sexy she was and start viewing her as his father's friend. Maybe that way he could keep his unruly body and imagination under control where she was concerned.

"Come on, Dad," he said, pushing the front door open. "Let's get you into bed."

"I don't want to lie down. I've been lying down all week."

"You need to take it easy. You don't want to tire yourself out."

"Plenty of time to rest when I'm dead."

His father stopped abruptly when he reached the living room.

"What have you done?" He turned to face Tyler, his eyes bright with dawning anger and outrage. "Where are all my things?"

"If you're talking about those moldering old newspapers you had piled up all over the place, I recycled them. They were a fire hazard and they made the house stink. Not to mention I found a nest of mice in one of the boxes."

"You had no right. Those were my papers. My property." His father was red in the face, the tendons showing in his neck.

"It was a bunch of useless junk. I have no idea why you were hanging on to them, anyway."

"For the crosswords."

Tyler blinked. Did his father have any idea how insane he sounded? He'd had years—*decades*—worth of newspapers stockpiled. Even if his father lived to be a hundred and fifty he'd never get around to all the crossword puzzles in those newspapers.

"Well, they're gone now. There's not much I can do about it, so you might as well get used to it."

As far as Tyler was concerned, the subject was closed. He turned away.

A hand clamped on to his forearm, the grip surprisingly strong.

"Don't you turn your back on me and walk away. Don't you dare disrespect me after all I've sacrificed for you."

His father was trembling with rage, the movement transmitted to Tyler through the grip on his arm. Spittle had formed at the corners of his father's mouth, and he had a look in his eye that Tyler recognized only too well.

Violence crackled in the air. It occurred to Tyler that if his father thought he could get away with it, he would have hit Tyler rather than simply grab him. Just like the old days.

Tyler opened his mouth to tell his father in no uncertain terms to get his hands off him.

"I've got vanilla cake, and a bit of chocolate fudge, so we can have some of both if you like."

Ally was standing inside the front door, silhouetted in the morning sunlight.

Tyler wondered how much she'd heard, what she'd seen. If she could feel the potential for violence vibrating in the air.

It took him a moment to find his voice. "Great. I'll put the kettle on."

He pushed his father's hand from his arm. It fell easily. He walked into the kitchen. He stopped in the center of the room, aware that he should be putting water in the kettle but unable to move beyond the sensation of his father's hand on his arm.

He'd come here intending to get his father settled at home, then get back to his life. But the next few days seemed to stretch before him unendingly.

Every time his father challenged him, every time he grew angry or sulky or demanding, Tyler was going to be staring down the past.

There was so much unresolved between them. So many ugly memories. So much unexpressed grief and outrage and anger.

For a split second the urge to damn duty to hell, to climb in his pickup and hit the road and leave his father to sort himself out was overwhelming. Tyler could almost taste the freedom and relief the decision would bring. He could go home, back to his life, and push all this crap into the dark corners again. Never to see the light of day.

A warm hand landed in the center of his back. Ally stood behind him, the plate of cake in hand.

"Tell me where everything is and I'll make some tea," she said quietly.

"You don't have to do that."

She didn't say anything, simply brushed past him and slid the plate onto the table. He watched as she filled the kettle and turned it on, then started rummaging in the cupboards for tea bags.

"Third cupboard on the left," he said after watching her search fruitlessly for a few seconds.

"Thanks."

He crossed the room and collected three mugs. He could smell Ally's vanilla-spice scent as he placed them in front of her.

She shot him an assessing glance. "You okay?"

"Yeah."

"You don't look okay. You look like you're about to pass out."

He frowned. "I've never fainted in my life."

For a moment the only sound in the kitchen was the sound of the kettle heating.

"You and your father really know how to push each other's buttons, huh?"

Tyler gave a small, humorless laugh. "You could say that."

He waited for her to say more, to probe, but she didn't. Instead, she sliced the cake and arranged the pieces on the plate. After a second, she put down the knife and looked at him.

"I want to say something about last night. I know this probably isn't the best time, but it's been bugging me, so I'm just going to spit it out."

"Okay." He turned to face her, leaning his hip against the counter and crossing his arms over his chest.

Her breasts lifted as she took a deep breath and launched into speech. "I meant it when I said I like you, Tyler. And I'd hate for what happened, or, more accurately, what didn't happen to stop us from being friends." Her expression was very earnest, which only made her look cuter than usual.

"Because I wanted to sleep with you and you said no?"

"Yes."

He filched a slice of cake. He took a bite, chewed and swallowed. Then he looked her in the eyes.

"I like you, too, Ally. And I'm happy to be friends. But you should probably know I'm still going to want to sleep with you." He shrugged apologetically. "It's kind of a one-way valve. Not really something I can turn on or off at the drop of a hat."

"Right." She seemed thrown by his directness. "Well, I guess I can handle that."

He ate the rest of the cake in one big bite. "Good," he said around his mouthful.

She smiled. "Nice manners."

He glanced at her curvy hips, shown to advantage by her skirt. "Nice skirt."

She slapped his hand away when he reached for another piece. "No cheating."

He knew she wasn't talking about the cake. "I'm only human."

Her gaze dropped to his chest, then his hips. "Tell me about it," she muttered, so quietly he almost didn't catch it. Then she grabbed the plate of cake. "Can you bring the tea in when it's ready?"

He watched her backside until she disappeared through the doorway to the living room.

He didn't understand her. There had been desire in her eyes when she looked at him. She wanted him, and she'd wanted him last night, too. And she'd stated boldly that she liked him. Yet she was determined to only be friends.

The kettle clicked off as it reached boiling point. He poured water into the mugs, automatically taking his father's tea bag out after a brief dunking. His father had always preferred a weak brew.

Tyler stilled when he registered what he'd done. He let out a small, heavy sigh.

A large part of him might want to drive off and leave his father to his own devices, but an even larger part seemed to be determined to do the right thing, no matter what the cost to himself or his peace of mind.

A couple of days, he reminded himself. *You can suck up almost anything for a couple of days.*

ALLY SWATTED A FLY AWAY from her face. She was sitting on one of the twin wooden sun loungers on Wendy's side deck, a glass of iced tea beside her, her notepad in hand, pondering how best to respond to Bankrupt Bridesmaid, a reader who was asking for advice on how to deal with a friend who had morphed into Bridezilla the moment her fiancé proposed.

Ally preferred to draft her responses to reader letters with pad and pencil, having learned long ago that her brain communicated best with the blank page via a pencil rather than a computer keyboard. Once she had her responses roughed out, she polished them at her laptop before emailing them into her editor.

Normally she loved questions like this—it gave her a chance to sound off against the ridiculous excesses of the modern wedding. During her tenure, Gertrude had developed a bit of a reputation for being tough on Bridezillas and young couples who seemed determined to start their married lives encumbered by the huge debt of a lavish, over-the-top wedding. Ally had handed out plenty of tough love in the form of column inches, but today she was having trouble concentrating.

The house next door was silent—no raised voices, no angry words floating over the fence—yet she couldn't forget the tension she'd witnessed between father and son this morning.

She'd heard the thwarted fury in Bob's voice, the shamed pride. She'd seen him grab his son's arm and, for a heartbeat, she'd thought he was going to strike Tyler.

And the expression on Tyler's face afterward when she'd followed him into the kitchen.

He'd looked so lost and desolate. The compulsion to wrap her arms around him had been so strong she'd nearly given in to it. She'd settled for simply placing a comforting hand on his back, as if she could somehow convey her sympathy and empathy to him through that single, small contact.

She'd like to offer him more. An ear to listen. A shoulder to cry on, if that was what he needed. Someone to vent to, a sounding board. Whatever he needed—and she sensed he desperately needed something, someone, on his side. But she wasn't about to foist herself on him. In the guise of Dear Gertrude she was happy to hand out guidance, but in real life Ally was much more inclined to hang back until asked. And her gut told her that Tyler would never ask. He was too self contained, too controlled. Too used to keeping his own counsel—or, perhaps, simply sucking it up and soldiering on.

Whatever. He hadn't asked for her comfort or advice or assistance, and she'd already volunteered enough. It was none of her business.

Forcing herself to focus, she began to write.

She'd barely composed a paragraph when the sound of a screen door slamming shut made her lift her head. It was Tyler, carrying a long roll of papers and what looked like a pencil case. He seemed frustrated as he stood on the top step, scanning the rear yard as though he were looking for an escape route.

For a few seconds she allowed herself to admire the hard strength of his body. He'd felt wonderful pressed against her last night—his big arms, his even bigger chest.

She told herself to stop ogling him the same moment he glanced over and caught her staring.

"Hey," he said.

"Hey. What's up?"

"Dad's sleeping. With the radio going full bore."

Her gaze dropped to the roll of papers in his hands and she guessed his dilemma. "Finding it hard to concentrate?"

"Just a little." His gaze shifted to scan the yard again. "I was thinking of trying the shed."

Ally turned her attention to the rusted metal structure that filled the corner of Bob's yard. Not exactly the most salubrious working environment on a hot summer day.

"Plenty of iced tea and peace and quiet over here, if you like," she offered before she could stop herself. "A spare lounger, too."

Tyler looked as though she'd thrown him a lifeline instead of a casual invitation. "I wouldn't be cramping your style?"

"I have precious little to cramp. Or hadn't you noticed?"

"In that case…"

He descended the steps and she lost sight of him behind the fence. She stood, ready to let him in the front door, then she heard the thunk of a boot connecting with wood and Tyler's head and torso appeared above the fence immediately in front of her.

"Would you mind grabbing these?"

He held out the roll of papers. She took them wordlessly. He gripped the pencil case in his teeth before slinging a leg over the fence and dropping to his feet on her side.

"Nothing like a shortcut," she said.

He took the papers from her. "Thanks for this."

"No problem." She waved a hand at the other seat. "You might want to check for bird poop before you sit."

"Thanks for the warning."

She went inside to collect a glass for him. When she returned, Tyler was toeing off his shoes and shedding his socks. She watched as he settled in a cross-legged position.

"Wow. You're pretty flexible for a guy."

She tried not to stare at the way his thigh muscles strained the soft denim of his jeans.

"Yoga."

He didn't really strike her as being a yoga kind of guy. Her skepticism must have shown on her face.

"I had a bit of back trouble a few years ago and my physiotherapist suggested it," Tyler explained. "It helps get the kinks out."

"I know. It's the only thing that keeps me mobile when I've spent a whole day writing."

She sank onto her lounger and reached for her notepad and pencil. Out of the corner of her eye she watched as Tyler unrolled the papers. A rough sketch of a sideboard filled the bulk of the first page and the margins were thick with notes, as well as angle calculations and measurements.

She dragged her attention to her own work and concentrated on encouraging Bankrupt Bridesmaid to show some spine in the face of the despotic bride-to-be, but she was very aware of Tyler working quietly beside her.

She was such a hypocrite. Just this morning, she'd offered him only friendship and reprimanded him when he made a comment about her skirt. Yet she couldn't even sit beside him for five minutes without becoming ridiculously aware of everything about him.

The play of light and shadow on his face.

The flickering muscles in his forearms as he made notations on his plans.

The clean, sunshiny smell of his clothing.

Maybe inviting him to share her peace and quiet hadn't been such a great idea after all.

"Is that your column you're working on?"

She glanced up from the doodle she'd been swirling along the bottom of the page to find Tyler watching her.

"Yep. Due tomorrow at lunchtime."

"Anything good?"

"An etiquette question about texting at the dinner table, an exploited bridesmaid. And there's one about a woman who is trying to decide if she should make contact with her birth mother or not. That's the toughest one."

"What do you think she should do?"

"I haven't answered that one yet."

"But you must have an idea what you're going to say."

She did. She fiddled with her pencil while she gathered her thoughts. "I think that family is important. That it strikes at the very root of who we are and who we think we are. If this woman is plagued by questions about her birth mother and her heritage, if it's stopping her from living her life to the fullest, then I think she should take the plunge."

"And what if she makes contact and it's not what she expected? What if there are no answers to her questions?"

"Then at least she'll know she tried. She can close the door and move on. At the moment, she's in limbo, unable to commit to making contact yet also unable to put it aside and get on with her life."

Tyler shook his head. "You have a tough job."

"Sometimes. But I can't imagine doing anything else now."

"You don't feel responsible? You never worry about what might happen if you say the wrong thing? Or if you don't answer a letter from someone desperate?"

"I read everything. Sometimes there are letters written by people who are clearly in crisis. I always respond with resources for them—counselors, support groups, whatever. But most letter writers are simply looking for impartial feedback, someone to call them on their bullshit or back up their instincts. They've got friends and family dumping their opinions, muddying the water. I'm the independent arbitrator."

"You're Judge Judy." Tyler said it with a small smile.

"With better hair. I hope."

"You sound like you love it."

"I do. I feel…I don't know…*connected* to these people. Like I really am their aunt Gertrude, and they're sitting across the table from me having a cup of tea and sharing their lives. I like to think that I help them. That I make a difference."

She was very aware of Tyler's gaze on her face as she finished. She gave a self-conscious laugh. "I know what you're thinking. I need to get a life, right?"

"Nothing wrong with enjoying what you do."

His hand smoothed over the blueprints as he spoke. She wondered if he was aware of the gesture or if it was unconscious.

"You enjoy what you do, too, don't you?"

"Yeah, I do," he said slowly. "It's easy to forget

that sometimes, dealing with clients and staff and deadlines, but I do."

"I know I'm not the best judge, since I don't actually own any furniture or have a home to put it in, but the pieces I saw on your website looked great. And really, really expensive."

His grin was unabashed. "Quality costs. What can I say?"

She found herself grinning in return.

She really liked this man. She liked his quiet confidence and his slow smile. She liked the way he seemed genuinely interested in her and what she had to say. She liked the fact that he'd made the decision to help his father, even though their relationship was clearly deeply troubled. She liked the way he'd kissed her last night. The way he'd pulled her onto his lap.

She realized she was staring at Tyler's mouth, and that he was watching her, a dark, smoky look in his silver eyes.

Danger, danger, Will Robinson.

"Speaking of quality, I'd better get this sorted or I'll be pushing it to make my deadline tomorrow," she said.

"Yeah, I've got a deadline I need to make, too."

They worked together for over an hour, talking occasionally, but mostly concentrating on their individual tasks. Given how disturbing she found Tyler on many levels, Ally was surprised by how easy it was to spend time with him. It was a warm day, but the breeze was cool and the iced tea even colder and he was good company—intelligent and perceptive and wry.

She felt a pang of regret when he started rolling up his papers. "Better go check on Dad."

She could see the new tension in him as he pulled on his socks.

"Anytime you need a break, come over."

She hesitated, all her admonitions to herself about interfering loud in her ears. Then she thought about that moment she'd witnessed this morning and threw caution to the wind. "Even if you just need to talk. Okay?"

Tyler was tugging on his shoes, but he flicked a quick look at her. "Thanks."

She bit her lip to stop herself from saying any more.

Tyler stood and gathered his things. "Thanks for sharing your peace and quiet. Hope I didn't distract you too much."

"You didn't distract me. It was nice having company for a change."

Especially his company.

He took their empty glasses inside. She watched him leave them in the kitchen sink before following him to the front door.

"Good luck with the nurse tomorrow," she said.

"Yeah. I have a feeling I'm going to need it, given Dad's reaction to the safety rails."

He surprised her then by leaning in and brushing

her lips with a brief kiss. "Bye, Ally, and thanks for saving my ass again today."

He started down the steps. Ally forced herself to close the door instead of standing there like a dodo watching him walk away again.

She could still feel the warm imprint of his lips on hers as she returned to the kitchen. Which was stupid, since it had been the barest peck. Nothing like the kisses they'd shared last night.

Those kisses had been enough to make her lose her head and crawl into his lap. Those kisses had kept her awake, staring at the ceiling.

She made an impatient noise, frustrated with herself. She crossed to the fridge and pulled the carton of Nuts About Chocolate from the freezer.

When in doubt, pig out.

A tried and true solution to many of life's problems. She hoped it worked as an antidote for unrequited lust.

Although the more she got to know Tyler, the less she suspected lust was her problem where he was concerned. Lust was all about pheromones and sweaty, carnal urges, but her attraction to Tyler was about a lot more than his body.

A dangerous acknowledgment.

She grabbed a spoon from the drawer and excavated herself a huge scoop of ice cream. Maybe by the time she'd dug her way to the bottom of the tub, she'd have unearthed some common sense.

CHAPTER SIX

TYLER WOKE TO FIND HIS father standing over him. He flinched, then immediately regretted the reflex. The last thing he wanted was for his old man to think Tyler was still afraid of him.

"What are you sleeping on the couch for?"

"I don't like the bed in my old room."

"There's nothing wrong with it."

"You sleep on it, then." Tyler swung his legs to the edge of the couch and rubbed the sleep from his eyes. He glanced at the clock on the mantle. Six-fifteen.

Great.

He estimated he'd had about three hours' rest between his father getting up and down and the lumpiness of the couch cushions.

"Stupid to sleep out here. Makes the place look messy. Your mother wouldn't like it."

Tyler gave his father an incredulous look. "But she would have loved the boxes of newspapers everywhere?"

His father frowned, unable to find a suitable response.

"What do you want for breakfast? Porridge? Toast?" Tyler asked.

He reached for the T-shirt he'd thrown over the arm of the couch last night and caught his father staring at the tattoo high on his left shoulder.

"Never thought a son of mine would get himself marked up like a common criminal."

"Porridge or toast?"

"Toast. I suppose."

"My pleasure," Tyler muttered as he headed for the kitchen.

He collected butter and jam from the fridge and slid two pieces of bread into the toaster.

"I used to sleep on that bed myself when your mother was sick."

His father was in the kitchen doorway, a stubborn expression on his face.

"What's that got to do with anything?"

"You said I should sleep in it. Well, I have, and it's fine. So I don't see why you have to muck up the living room."

Tyler sighed. "Just drop it, okay?"

"It's a perfectly good bed—"

"Bloody hell, will you drop it?" The sharp crack of his voice echoed in the room.

"Don't you raise your voice at me. I asked you a perfectly legitimate question. The least you can do is answer it when you're staying under my roof."

Tyler smiled grimly. How many times had he heard that as a kid? *When you're under my roof.*

He nailed his father with a look. "You want an

answer? How about this—maybe I don't like the memories in there."

It was the closest Tyler had ever come to directly addressing the history between them. His father stiffened. For a moment they stared at each other across the kitchen.

His father was the first to break the contact, glancing away and shuffling toward the table. "I like honey on my toast."

Tyler opened his mouth to push the issue—his father was the one who'd kept on about the bloody bed, after all. Then he saw the tremor in his father's hands as he clasped them in front of him.

Being old and sick doesn't let him off the hook.

The toaster popped. Tyler closed his eyes for a long moment. Years of resentment pressed against his sternum, wanting out.

He opened his eyes and crossed to the pantry to collect the honey. He slid it onto the table and went back to grab the toast. The plate rattled as he dumped it in front of his father.

Then he strode for the door. He took the steps in two bounds. The grass was cold and dewy on his bare feet as he hit the lawn and kept walking. He didn't stop until he was standing in front of the overgrown mess that used to be his mother's vegetable patch.

He should have said something. He should go inside right now and confront that bastard. Ask why. Demand to know what kind of a man took out his petty frustrations on his own children.

Tyler didn't move.

He dropped his head, pinching the bridge of his nose.

He didn't understand what was holding him back from the confrontation. It wasn't simply his father's frailty. There was something else, something dark and heavy that stopped Tyler every time he felt the urge to lay it all out in the open.

For some reason, he thought of Ally as he stared at the ground. Remembered the way she'd placed her hand so calmly and surely on his back yesterday. That small, simple human contact had grounded him. Reminded him that there was a world outside of this childhood house of terror.

He lifted his head and looked toward her place. She'd said he should come by if he needed a break. Or if he needed to talk.

He imagined himself going next door, knocking on the door. She'd probably still be in bed, and she'd answer with her hair mussed, soft and warm. He imagined himself kissing her, taking her to her bed and making love with her until he forgot about his father and all the unhappiness of the past.

Making love with Ally would be like that, he sensed. All-consuming. Nothing else would matter.

He rubbed the back of his neck, turning away from Ally's. She'd made herself more than clear. She wanted to be friends. She'd hardly appreciate him turning up on her doorstep at six in the morning, forcing the issue.

He walked back to the house. The kitchen was empty—his father had dumped his plate in the sink. Tyler cleaned up, putting the honey and butter away, rinsing the plate. Then he went to check on his father.

He wasn't in the living room, or his bedroom. Then Tyler heard the sound of running water and swore.

Yesterday, he'd covered the rules with his father. No showers without assistance. Even with the safety rails, the shower was a dangerous place for a man in his late seventies, fresh from major surgery.

Tyler should have known that his father wouldn't listen. Robert was bloody-minded at the best of times, and it obviously chaffed him hugely to have Tyler in a position of authority over him.

Tyler stopped outside the bathroom door and knocked. "How are you doing in there?" he called.

He waited, but there was no reply.

"Dad. Are you okay?"

Again, no reply.

Tyler tried the handle and the door swung open. The bathroom was thick with steam, the mirrors foggy with condensation.

"Dad. Are you all right?"

"Go away. Can't a man shower in peace?"

The tension left Tyler's shoulders. "What's wrong with you? Couldn't you hear me calling?" He was annoyed now that he'd been worried.

"I said go away." There was a quavering note to his father's voice.

Tyler frowned. Reaching out, he slid the shower door open.

His father was sitting in the shower seat, water pummeling the wall to his left. He had a bloody gash on his shin and a red mark on his forehead and was gripping the arms of the chair like grim death.

"What happened?" Tyler asked, leaning in to turn the taps off.

"Stupid chair tripped me up. Banged my head."

His father was gray, all the color leached from his face. Blood dripped from the cut on his shin, swirling toward the drain in crimson ribbons.

Tyler looked around and saw that his father hadn't thought to bring a towel into the bathroom with him.

"Give me a second." He darted out of the bathroom and grabbed a towel from the cupboard in the hallway. Reentering the room, he saw his father hadn't moved, his grip still white knuckled on the chair. Tyler draped the towel over the wall rack and faced his father.

"Here. Put your hands on my shoulders. I'll help you stand."

Tyler bent over his father. His father's mouth worked. Tyler waited for him to object, to tell him to go to hell. But after a moment his father released his grip on the chair and leaned forward, reaching for Tyler's shoulders. Tyler waited until his father had a solid hold before wrapping both arms around his father's back.

"We'll stand on three, okay? One, two, three."

He tightened his grip and shifted his weight. He could feel his father's ribs beneath his hands, could feel the quiver of straining muscles as his father tried to stand. A few tense seconds later, his father was wavering on his feet, his breath coming in harsh gasps as he clung to Tyler's shoulders.

For a long moment they remained locked in an unintentional embrace, son supporting father. Tyler couldn't help but be profoundly, viscerally aware of his father's frailty. His nakedness, the papery thinness of his skin, the lack of substance to the body in his arms.

Despite everything, compassion stirred within him.

His father needed Tyler, and it made him ashamed and scared and vulnerable. No matter what had happened between them in the past, Tyler couldn't stop himself from responding to that vulnerability.

He'd thought he was here for himself, so he could look himself in the eye and know he'd done the right thing. Standing in this house, his father trembling in his arms, Tyler understood that his motivation was far more complex and conflicted than simple duty. There were bonds tying them together that went beyond rational words and thoughts.

He wasn't sure it was a welcome realization.

"How are you doing?" he asked.

"I can stand on my own."

"Grab the rail, then," Tyler said gruffly.

Only when his father had transferred his grip to the safety rail did Tyler release him and step backward.

"I'm okay. I can take it from here." His father's voice was shaky, but Tyler didn't doubt his determination.

"I'll be in the hall if you need me."

Tyler exited, putting a few paces between them. He pulled his phone from his pocket and called Gabby in Melbourne.

She picked up on the third ring.

"I'm going to need longer than a week," he said.

ALLY KEPT HER DISTANCE for the next few days. She left some caramel slice on the doorstep on the first day, and some new crossword-puzzle books for Bob on the third. She felt guilty about not visiting him in person, especially since she'd seen him almost every day when he was in hospital. She guessed he was probably wondering where she was, but she felt the need to put some distance between herself and Tyler after their afternoon on her deck. He was too interesting, too sexy, too compelling—and she was only human.

The two houses were so close that it was impossible for her ignore the nurse coming and going each day—once in the morning, once in the evening—and she was very aware of the fact that Tyler's pickup was still parked on the street, day after day.

Perhaps she'd gained the wrong impression, but she'd been certain that he'd planned on being in Woodend for only a few days. Already those "few days" were stretching into a week.

She was changing the bed on the afternoon of the fifth day when she caught sight of Tyler through the window. He was visible for a few seconds as he crossed the sidewalk in front of Wendy's house. She was in the middle of tucking the top sheet in, but she froze, holding her breath. Sure enough, ten seconds later she heard the low thrum of his truck starting. It flashed briefly into view as he drove down the street. Then he was gone.

She abandoned the bed on the spot, hustling into the study to grab her letter folder, then stopping in the kitchen to collect the chocolate-chip cookies she'd made that morning. She was outside and climbing the steps to Bob's place within minutes of Tyler's departure.

A plump blond woman in her early forties answered the door to Ally's knock. She wasn't in uniform, but Ally guessed she must be Bob's nurse.

"Hi, I'm Ally from next door. I was wondering if Bob was up for a visit?"

"I'm Belinda, and I think he'd be thrilled to see you. Especially with those cookies in hand."

"He does have a bit of a sweet tooth."

The other woman stepped back. Ally shot a furtive

glance to check the street was still clear of Tyler's vehicle before entering. And immediately felt foolish. So what if he came home? It wasn't as though she was going to jump his bones while his father and the nurse looked on.

Bob was sitting in the armchair in the living room when she entered, one of his puzzle books open in his lap.

"Hello, there. I thought you might like a visit and something to go with your cup of tea," she said.

Bob glanced up. "Been wondering where you'd got to."

Ally tried not to squirm with guilt. "I had a couple of tight deadlines I needed to hit," she fibbed.

Bob grunted. "That's what Tyler said it'd be."

"Can I bribe my way back into your good books with a cookie?"

"Nobody needs to bribe anybody. Just pointing out that you were missed, that's all."

It was said gruffly, with Bob scowling at his puzzle, but from a self-contained man like him it was the equivalent of a Shakespearian sonnet and Ally couldn't help but be touched.

"I'm sorry," she said sincerely. "I promise not to be a stranger, okay?"

Even if that meant seeing Tyler more often than was advisable for her sanity and peace of mind.

"Fair enough."

"So is that a yes to a cookie?"

As they snacked she helped Bob finish his

crossword puzzle before reading him a few of her letters, since he seemed to get a kick out of them.

They were debating the merits of modern versus old-fashioned manners when Ally noted Bob checking his watch for the third time in as many minutes.

"I'm not keeping you from anything, am I, Bob?"

She didn't want to mess up his routine with her impromptu visit.

"Just wondering where Tyler's gotten to. He said he was only going to be twenty minutes."

Ally tensed. She'd been visiting with Bob for almost forty minutes, which meant Tyler could return at any moment. Even though she was aware that it made her an enormous coward, she shot out of her seat and started gathering her things.

"I should really get back. Today's cleaning day, and I've got a whole bunch of rooms to dust and Mr. Whiskers needs to be brushed."

Bob blinked. "Well, okay. But I'm going to hold you to what you said—don't be a stranger."

"I won't. I promise."

She bent and kissed his cheek. Then she beat a retreat to the door. Feeling every inch the yellow-belly she was, she breathed a sigh of relief as she descended the steps.

Phew.

Then she saw a flash of red at the end of the street. Sure enough, it was Tyler's pickup.

She swallowed. Any second now he would be

parking, getting out of his truck and looking at her with those devastating silver eyes of his. And every good intention she'd formed over the past few days would dissolve like butter on a hot griddle.

She didn't stop to think, she simply scampered down the path like a frightened rabbit, bolted across the few feet of sidewalk that separated the two houses, then scampered up Wendy's path and onto her porch.

She fumbled the key, her heart thumping like a kettledrum beneath her breastbone. She heard Tyler's truck pull up, heard the engine stop. Any second now he'd be out of the truck and—

The door opened and she slipped inside and shut it behind her. She stood with her back pressed against the wood, waiting for the adrenaline to wash through her system.

What is wrong with you?

It was a damned good question. When had she gone from being content to be Tyler's friend to being afraid to spend time with him? When had she become so scared of her own feelings and impulses that she was literally barricading herself from temptation?

She didn't know. All she knew was that she wanted to be sensible where Tyler was concerned—and she was terribly afraid that she didn't have the willpower to carry it through.

She groaned, lifting the file in her hands to bang it against her forehead. She was such a mess. Not many women would be bending themselves into emotional pretzels because the sexy, available, lovely, funny, gentle guy next door was interested in them. In fact, most other women would be skipping through the day, delighted by the prospect.

But most other women had something to offer a man like Tyler, and Ally didn't. She was a guaranteed disaster, a walking, talking disappointment waiting to happen.

She walked slowly up the hall and threw her folder onto the desk in the study. Then she wandered into the living room, feeling dazed and oddly bereft, as though she'd abandoned something important and priceless. Which was nuts, given that twenty seconds ago she'd been panting with relief because she'd avoided encountering Tyler on the street.

She found herself on the deck, the sun bright overhead. She stared blankly at the garden and the deep blue sky.

Maybe she really was going nuts. Maybe she should resign as Dear Gertrude and stop perpetrating the fraud that she knew anything about anything.

The hard thwack of a screen door shutting made her start. Her head snapped around and she found herself staring at Tyler as he stood on the steps on the other side of the fence.

They looked at each other for a long, drawn out moment. Ally's heartrate picked up, the beat pounding in the pit of her belly.

"Have I done something wrong?" Tyler asked.

"No. Of course not."

"Then why are you avoiding me?"

"I'm not avoiding you," she lied.

"So why didn't you bring the caramel slice in the other day instead of leaving it on the doorstep? And why did you bolt when you saw my truck?"

Because I'm a certifiable nutbag. Because you confuse and scare and challenge the hell out of me. Because I want something that I know can only end one way—badly.

"Because."

She meant to say more, offer him some kind of face-saving lie, but the words wouldn't come. Maybe it was the way he was watching her so intently, the clear light in his eyes demanding the truth. Or maybe she was simply sick of hiding—from herself, and him.

She sighed. "Okay. I was avoiding you," she admitted.

"I thought we were going to be friends."

"We were. I mean, we are."

"You avoid your other friends like this?"

"No."

He cocked his head, considering. "I'm not sure if I should be encouraged or insulted."

There was something very…warm about the way he said it. And the way his gaze raked her body briefly before settling on her face again.

A dart of something close to panic raced down her spine. "Definitely you shouldn't feel encouraged."

"So it was an insult, then?"

She stared at him. Why was he making it so hard for her to be sensible and do the right thing?

"You know it wasn't."

"I told you I wanted to sleep with you. You said you could handle it."

"I thought I could."

"Now *that* I'm definitely taking as encouragement." Tyler started down the steps.

"What are you doing?" she squeaked, even though she already knew the answer.

"Coming over the fence."

"I don't think that's a good idea."

"I do."

She heard the thud as his boot found the first cross support. His head and shoulders appeared above the fence.

"Tyler. Stop. This is a bad idea."

"It's a great idea. The best idea I've had in weeks."

He slung his leg over the fence. Ally could feel her heart leaping around in her chest, whether from excitement or panic she had no idea. She told herself to move but her feet felt as though they were set in cement.

You want this. Don't pretend you don't.

And she did, more than anything. But Tyler had enough pain in his life right now and she didn't want to hurt him.

He landed on the deck with a thump, knees bent to absorb the shock. He straightened to his full height and took a step toward her.

She took a step backward. "I told you the other night. This is a mistake."

"Doesn't feel like a mistake." He took another step forward.

She took one backward. "We like each other too much."

His eyebrows rose. "Since when has that ever been a problem?"

He took another step. When she tried to back away again, he reached out and grabbed her shoulder.

"You just ran out of maneuvering room."

She glanced back and saw that she'd been about to collide with the French doors. She turned to look into his eyes.

"I guess that means I'm officially cornered."

"I guess it does."

He closed the final distance that separated them, pulling her close. His head lowered toward her, but at the last moment she twisted her face to the side so that his mouth found the soft skin beneath her ear instead of her lips.

A wave of need washed through her as he opened his mouth against her neck.

"If this happens, it means nothing," she said.

Tyler's tongue swirled against her skin, his mouth sucking lightly. "You don't know that."

"I do, because that's the only way this is going to happen. It has to be a one-off, a roll in the hay." She wondered if he could hear the thread of desperation beneath her words as clearly as she could. "No promises, no tomorrow. Just sex."

She clenched her hands at her sides to stop herself from grabbing him. If he agreed to her conditions, she would let herself touch him. But until then he was as off-limits as he'd always been.

"Maybe you should wait until afterward before you make any binding decisions." His words were a whisper across her skin.

"You're not listening to me. It doesn't matter how good it is or how I feel or how you feel. This can only ever be one night."

He must have heard the certainty in her tone because he pulled back a few inches to look into her face.

"You're serious, aren't you?"

"Yes. Absolutely. You think I'm playing hard to get?"

"To be honest, I don't know. But I know you want this as much as I do."

There was no point denying it, not when she was practically boneless with longing from a few simple kisses to her neck.

"Not everything we want is good for us."

She could see him sifting through their conversation, assessing her words and warnings in a new light. After a long beat, his grip loosened and he stepped away.

"I don't understand."

"I told you. I don't want to start something when

it has nowhere to go. I'm here for a few more weeks, and then I'm leaving. No matter what."

He frowned.

"So if you want to have sex, we can. As long as we both understand that it's not the beginning of something else," she said.

Tyler looked at her for a long beat. Then his gaze slid away from her to focus somewhere behind her. She knew what his answer would be. He was a man who spent hours carving a piece of wood into perfection. He didn't do things by halves.

"I want more than sex," he said.

So do I. That's the craziest thing of all. I want to wake in your arms. I want to laugh with you. I want to talk to you and learn about you. I want to ease your pain and comfort you.

"That's all that I can give you."

His gaze was intense when it returned to her. "You're the one who said this kind of thing doesn't happen every day."

"I'm trying to be smart here, Tyler. I'm trying to do the right thing."

He looked as though he wanted to say more, to ask more, but he didn't. Instead, he took a step away from her.

He had too much pride to talk her into sleeping with him. Which was just as well, because her resistance was paper-thin at best.

She smoothed her hands down the front of her thighs.

"Bob's nurse seems nice," she said brightly. "How's he getting along with her?"

It took Tyler a moment to change gears and follow her lead. "He seems to like her. And she's good at handling him."

"I noticed that. He seems stronger, too."

"Yeah. He's moving around more easily."

"I guess you'll be heading back to Melbourne soon."

"Actually, I've decided to stay on. See things through." He said the words casually, as though it wasn't a big deal. As though committing to care for his father through his final days barely merited a mention.

"That's a big change of plans," she said carefully.

"Yeah."

He didn't say any more, as usual. Not for the first time, she fought the urge to grab him by the shirtfront and shake him until some of the thoughts and feelings he held so tightly to his chest were knocked loose. But she was hardly in a position to demand anything from him, having done her damnedest to keep him at arm's length.

"If you need anything. If there's anything I can do…"

Tyler looked at her, and she knew exactly what he was thinking, what he wanted. "Thanks. I'll keep it in mind."

They were back to polite distance again. She told herself it was a good thing, even if it felt wrong.

"I told your father I'd be over more regularly. So I'll probably see you tomorrow."

Tyler nodded. He glanced toward the fence. "Suppose I'd better go start dinner."

She watched as he climbed the fence. A part of her still couldn't believe she was letting him go. But she was. And it was the right thing.

She waited until he'd disappeared inside before closing the French doors behind her and retreating to the couch. Her magazine subscriptions had arrived for the month, forwarded, as usual, with the rest of her mail by the *Herald*. She picked up *Vogue Living*, keen to anesthetize and distract herself with other people's beautiful homes.

But even as she flicked through glossy pages filled with designer decors and the latest homewares, she was cognizant of an echoing hollowness inside herself. It took her a moment to identify the feeling as loneliness.

She smiled a little grimly. *Get used to that feeling, girlfriend.*

It was better to be lonely than to hurt people. She believed that in her bones. She'd seen her mother ruin too many men—and women—to think anything else.

Most memorable was Tony, the Spaniard who'd married her mother then spent six years chasing her around the world, trying to keep her love. He'd been a wreck at the end, confused and despairing over her mother's declaration that while she loved him passionately, she would never live with him again.

Then there had been Dawn, the young artist who'd been so enamored of her mother's fire and charisma she'd put her own art aside to devote herself to being her mother's assistant—only to be cast aside when her mother inevitably grew bored with her. Dawn had attempted suicide in the aftermath of Ally's mother's abandonment, she'd been so bereft and disillusioned.

At the time, Ally had been furious with her mother for not rushing straight to Dawn's side. She'd called her mother callous and unfeeling and selfish. But that was before she'd left her own trail of wreckage in London and Sydney and Los Angeles, just as cruelly abandoning the people who loved her.

• Who was she to judge her mother, after all, when she was made in the same mold?

She turned another page in the magazine.

She'd done the right thing. Definitely she had.

THAT NIGHT, TYLER SAT at the kitchen table and tried to concentrate on his design drawings instead of the racket in the living room and the one-track record in his head.

His father was watching television, the volume through the roof, as usual. And Tyler couldn't stop thinking about Ally.

It wasn't simply because she'd rejected him. Sure,

he had a healthy ego, same as the next guy, and it stung a little to be dismissed so easily. But it wasn't pique that kept her in his thoughts.

He couldn't work her out. The visits to his father, the caramel slice, the way she'd appointed herself his father's champion and confronted Tyler on his father's behalf—they were all the acts of a caring, generous, nurturing person. And yet she wasn't prepared to give the connection between them a chance to become something more than sexual attraction and a whole lot of like.

A few years ago, Tyler would have taken up her no-strings-sex offer and run with it. He would have taken her to bed and explored every inch of her body and walked away the next morning with no regrets. But he was thirty-seven years old, and he'd been around enough to know when something had the potential to be good. He didn't want a single night. He didn't want to explore only Ally's body, he wanted to explore her mind, the person who looked out at him through those warm brown eyes. He wanted to start something that had no end date. Something with a future.

Ally, on the other hand, had made it very, very clear that she wasn't interested in pursuing any connection that might develop into a relationship. She was leaving in a few weeks time. *No matter what.*

Tyler rested his elbows on the table, reflecting that if a mate came to him and told him the same story about a woman he was hooked on, Tyler would have no hesitation in labeling the woman Too Much Trouble.

Ally *was* too much trouble. She looked at him with naked desire, then held him at arm's length and told him he could have only so much and no more. She offered him friendship and comfort and understanding, but refused to consider anything else.

Like he said, too much trouble. Yet here he sat, literally unable to get her out of his thoughts.

You're officially a sad sack, buddy.

In the living room, his father's voice rose briefly above the din of the television. No doubt he was yelling at a contestant on one of the many game shows he loved to watch. There was no point asking if his father would mind reducing the volume to a more sociable level—Tyler had already tried that three times. Each time his father grudgingly reduced the sound, only for it to creep up in increments until it was once again making the windows vibrate in their frames.

He was rubbing his forehead and contemplating the purchase of a pair of really efficient noise canceling earphones when his phone rang, sending the handset buzzing across the kitchen table. The number on the screen had too many digits to be anything other than an international call.

"Jon," he said as he took the call.

There was a short pause before his brother spoke. "You psychic or something?"

"No, I have caller I.D."

"Right."

"What's up?"

"You didn't get back to me about Dad."

Tyler sat back in his chair. "You said you didn't care. Actually, you said you didn't give a shit."

"Yeah, well. Guess I'm not immune to guilt after all. How is he?"

"Improving. He's been out of hospital for six days now."

"So he's going to be okay?"

"Not in the long-term. The cancer's metastasized. It's in his liver, his kidneys. Everywhere, basically."

Silence while Jon chewed this over.

"How long have they given him?"

"Months, maybe only weeks. You know what they're like with those kinds of things. Lots of talk about how unpredictable it is."

"Right."

Tyler heard the scratch of a cigarette lighter. "You still smoking?"

"I quit three years ago."

His brother inhaled audibly on the other end of the line. Really sucking the nicotine in.

"I thought you were going to see him then bugger off?" Jon said.

"So did I. But it turns out you're not the only one who's not immune to guilt."

"So, what? You're sticking it out?"

"Yeah."

"Why?"

"Honestly? I don't know. You want to talk to him?"

"No."

There was no mistaking the vehemence in his brother's tone.

"Sorry," Jon said after a moment. "I just... I don't want to talk to him." He laughed, the sound empty and hollow. "Wish I'd got a bloody letter from a solicitor or something, telling me it was all over, to be honest."

Tyler understood that sentiment only too well. "What do you want, then?"

"I don't know."

Tyler imagined his brother pacing restlessly. Jon had always found it hard to sit still for long, especially when he was agitated.

"I could keep you updated. Send you a text every now and then, let you know what's happening," Tyler offered.

His brother swore softly under his breath. Tyler knew what Jon was thinking, how he was feeling. The push and pull of guilt and anger. The desire to punish, the need for closure.

"Yeah. Okay," Jon said after a moment. "Let me know how he's doing." He sounded resigned. Pissed with himself. Another emotion Tyler was familiar with.

"Anything else you need?"

"Sure—less snow and about half a dozen more decent contractors."

"How's business?"

"Too good. Too bloody busy."

"Not a bad way to be."

"No. Listen, I gotta go."

"Okay. I'll let you know if anything changes."

"Thanks."

Tyler ended the call and picked up his pencil again but didn't immediately return to work.

Jon had always been the tough one, the hard one. So there was a strange comfort in knowing that his brother was as torn by their father's illness as he was.

Tyler turned his attention to his blueprints. The noise from the next room grew louder as his father changed channels. Tyler spent another ten minutes trying to tune it out before giving up. Standing, he gathered his things and exited the house.

He glanced briefly next door as he descended the rear steps. If things were different between him and Ally, if he hadn't misread that look in her eyes this afternoon and climbed the fence and tried to kiss her, he could go over there now and seek sanctuary.

But he had, which meant he couldn't throw himself on her mercy again.

He made his way across the yard to the shed. The double doors rattled noisily as he pushed them wide. He flicked on the overhead light. The smell of damp wood and old oil hit him as he surveyed the jumbled mess.

When he and Jon were kids, this place had been strictly off-limits unless they were accompanied by their father. Every tool had had its home on the Peg-

Board on the wall, lumber had been stored neatly in the overhead racks, and precisely labeled shelves had housed his father's many power tools.

A far cry from the shambles of today.

Tyler wondered why he was surprised—the house had been a disaster, after all—but somehow he was. This shed had always been his father's domain. His fiefdom. The place where he was most in charge of the world. And now it was a chaos of stacked boxes and grimy engine parts and old paint cans and moldy camping gear and rusty garden equipment.

Tyler almost returned to the house, but the memory of the blaring television was enough to make him stay. He needed to get some work done.

He dusted the top of a nearby carton and dumped his papers on it, then rearranged some of the junk. If he could clear the decks enough, he could use a couple of boxes as a work surface in the short-term, and in the long-term he could make a quick trip to Melbourne to grab his portable drafting table. It would be hotter than hell inside the tin shed during the day, but he figured it would cool down quickly enough at night with the doors open. Enough for him to have several hours of quiet and privacy to work in. Several very necessary hours if he was to maintain the design side of the business while taking this extended leave of absence.

He'd almost cleared a viable space when he shifted a stack of boxes and found an old table, draped with a paint-spattered sheet. It was too small to be any use to him, but something about the height and scale of the piece gave him pause.

Many years ago when he'd first finished his apprenticeship he'd made a side table for his mother. It had been a chance for him to show off his skills in marquetry and he'd spared no effort in creating an elaborate pattern in the round mahogany tabletop. He'd given it to his mother on Mother's Day with more than a little pride. She'd been flatteringly pleased with the gift, although, as always, she hadn't been able to resist one of her habitual backhanded digs. *It's beautiful, Tyler—but, of course, I have to say that. I'm your mother.*

Tyler had been too preoccupied over the past few days to register that the table had not been on display in the house. And perhaps it wasn't a huge surprise that his father had relegated it to the shed. He'd hardly welcome having a constant reminder of his estranged son cluttering his home.

Tyler tugged the sheet from the table. It had been a long time since he'd looked at any of his earlier pieces. No doubt he'd be embarrassed by how derivative the design was. If his memory served him, he'd taken many of his design cues from a classic Chippendale table. And he'd gone a little crazy with the marquetry, determined to impress his mother.

The sheet slid free. Tyler went very still.

It was his table, but in name only. The height, the shape were still the same, but the carefully polished circular top was now a scarred mess of chewed-up wood. Saw marks marred the rim in several places and nail holes pitted the surface, destroying the delicate inlay of satinwood, cherry and beech. Indentations marked where a hammer had smashed the wood, compressing the timber in regular circles. A large symmetrical gouge bit deeply into the wood on the far side. It took Tyler a few seconds to recognize it as the imprint a portable bench vise left behind when it had been clamped in place for a long time.

When he'd first started his own business, he'd taken on some restoration and insurance work to see him through the lean times. He'd seen pieces that had been left outside in the weather, mauled by pets, damaged by hot dishes and cigarettes and solvents. He'd seen scratches and gouges and breaks. But he'd never seen willful, intentional, extensive damage like this. This was...brutal.

There was no other word for it.

His father had destroyed the table. Systematically, deliberately. He'd taken a finely crafted piece of furniture—a labor of love that Tyler had offered to his mother—and turned it into a common workbench. He'd hacked at it, pounded it, scarred it. Then he'd cast it aside, his mission complete.

Tyler rested his hands on the marred surface, feeling the rough edges and pits beneath his fingers, trying to understand. Trying to get his head around the kind of vindictiveness, the malice, that it would take to do this to a once-beautiful piece of furniture.

Was it jealousy that had driven the man? Hate? Resentment that Tyler had given the table to his mother instead of his father? Anger?

But it was beyond him. Tyler simply couldn't comprehend the mind of a man who would wreak such senseless damage. Just as he'd never been unable to understand a man who would torture a family pet to punish his own child.

His father was a monster.

The thought drove him out of the shed toward the house. The door hit the wall hard as he entered. He strode straight to the living room and yanked the television plug out of the wall, silencing the deafening roar.

His father opened his mouth to protest.

Tyler took a step toward him, his hands fisted. "Why'd you do it?"

"What are you talking about? Put my show back on."

"The table. Why'd you destroy it?"

His father scowled. "The kitchen table? There's nothing wrong with it." But his gaze shifted to the side nervously.

"Don't pretend you don't know what I'm talking about, you nasty old bastard." Tyler was shaking with fury, barely able to contain himself.

"I don't have to listen to this. Not in my own home." His father started pushing himself out of his chair.

"You're not going anywhere, not until you tell me

why. Why you ruined that table and why you smacked the hell out of me and Jon when we were kids."

His father's head snapped back as though Tyler had slapped him.

"I never hit you," his father said with absolute conviction.

It was Tyler's turn to flinch. In all the years and all the times he'd envisioned this conversation, not once had he imagined his father denying the plain truth of history.

"You used to smack us around all the time. You gave Jon a bloody nose and perforated my eardrum. You beat him down the hallway with the buckle end of your belt."

"You two smashed the light on the porch with your yahooing around."

"*We were kids.* We were mucking around."

"You were out of control."

Tyler shook his head. "What about Mom? Every night you used to scream at her in the kitchen."

His father's jaw jutted angrily. "Thirty-seven and you're not even married. What would you know? All the time I spent trying to make ends meet, trying to stop you two from getting in trouble and not one single word of thanks. You've got your own business, your brother's in Canada. You're both doing well. And not one word of thanks."

Bob drew himself to his full height. In his expression was the volcanic rage of Tyler's childhood. A lifetime of memories flashed through Tyler's mind, a slide show of misery—his mother in tears, Jon cowering from their father's blows, the sound of his own fear as his father laid into him. Over and over, the memories kept coming.

"You can't rewrite history," Tyler said, his voice low and hard. "You got stuck into us every chance you got."

Something in his father's face shifted. "You don't know what you're talking about. My father used to knock me from one side of the house to the other. And you two got a couple of smacks." His father's mouth worked for a second and he swallowed noisily. *"I loved you boys."*

His father turned his back abruptly and took a shuddering breath. Tyler heard something click in his father's throat.

Then, his shoulders very square, his father walked slowly from the room, across the hallway and into his bedroom. The door swung shut between them.

Tyler was left standing alone. Adrenaline still surged through his body, but the fight was over.

And he had no idea who'd won.

CHAPTER SEVEN

ALLY KNEW THAT SOMETHING was wrong the moment she opened the door. Tension radiated off Tyler's big body in waves and his face was set like stone. Everything about him screamed wounded, angry animal.

"Tyler. What happened?"

"Can I come in? Just for a few minutes."

"Of course." She ushered him inside. "I was just about to open a bottle of wine."

She'd actually been in the middle of a yoga session, but she'd never seen a man more in need of a drink in her life.

She led him to living room, then ducked into the kitchen. She gathered two glasses and a bottle of red wine, her mind racing.

He and Bob must have had another fight. She couldn't think of any other explanation for the tight, hard expression on Tyler's face.

She added a packet of crackers to her haul, in case Tyler hadn't eaten. Then she took a deep breath and joined him.

He was standing in front of the French doors, his

gaze bouncing around as though he didn't quite know what to do with himself.

She didn't say a word, simply opened the wine and poured him a glass.

"Here. You look like you could do with this."

He glanced down, then reached out and wrapped his fingers around the bowl of the glass. "Thanks."

She watched as he tipped his head back and downed half the wine in one swallow. Another tip of his head and the glass was empty.

She sank into the cushions of the couch, her knees drawn to her chest. Waiting.

Tyler stared at his empty glass for a long moment. A muscle flickered in his jaw as though he was clenching and unclenching his teeth. The room was so silent she could hear the clock ticking and the hum of the refrigerator in the next room.

Finally, he looked at her. "He used to beat us."

She took a deep breath. Nodded. "I wondered."

It had been a dark, unvoiced possibility in the back of her mind ever since she'd witnessed that moment between father and son the morning Bob came home from hospital.

"Did you? Funny. All those years, and not a single teacher ever asked about the bruises. None of the neighbors, either."

"Some people don't want to see."

He wandered to the bookcase. She watched as he picked up and put down the small trinkets Wendy had displayed there.

"Everyone used to think he was a great guy. Good old Bob Adamson, a man you could rely on. Honest, hardworking, reliable. A regular saint." He looked across the room at her, his eyes a dark, turbulent gray. "You like him. You think he's a nice old man."

She nodded. "Yes. I did."

"He was a bastard. What he did to me and Jon…" Tyler shook his head.

She shifted to grab the bottle. "Pass me your glass."

She poured more wine then returned the glass.

"Thanks."

He drank a mouthful. Then sat on the edge of the cushion of the armchair opposite her, his elbows on his knees, both hands cradling his drink.

His posture was so tight, so protective, every instinct urged her to go wrap her arms around him. She forced herself to remain seated. As much as this man needed comfort, she sensed that the words he was slowly, painfully doling out had been sitting inside him for years. More than anything right now, he needed to talk.

"When I left here, I never wanted to see him again. I tried to stay away, but after a few years I realized I couldn't do it to Mom. So I saw them once a year, on her birthday, until she died. And then I figured I was off the hook. It was over, and I'd finally escaped."

"And then I came to see you."

"Then you came. And I told myself I didn't give a shit that he was sick, that he was dying. But I couldn't stop thinking about it, so I decided that I'd come and say my piece—all the things I'd never said to him. Get it off my chest once and for all. Then we really would be done." He shook his head in disgust.

"What happened?"

"I couldn't do it." He flicked a glance at her. "I walked into his hospital room, ready to give it to him… He looked so old. So *small*. And I couldn't do it. So I figured I'd just walk away, leave it at that. But I couldn't do that, either." He sounded so angry with himself.

"You think that's a bad thing?"

"He knocked me and Jon around every chance he got. Told me I was no good and I'd never amount to anything more times than I could count. Even when he was decent, I was scared of him, waiting for the other shoe to drop. So, yeah, I think that's a bad thing."

"I don't think compassion is ever a bad thing."

He shook his head, rejecting her words.

She abandoned her casual posture and shifted to the edge of her seat. "Something happened tonight."

"No, it didn't." He laughed, a hard, sharp sound. "All those years I imagined sticking it to him. Looking him in the eye and telling him what he was. And nothing happened."

Ally was struggling to keep up. "You finally confronted him? That's what happened tonight?"

"Yeah. I was out in the shed, trying to find quiet

to work in. I cleared away some old junk and I found a table I'd made for my mother when I finished my apprenticeship."

He took a big gulp of the wine before continuing. "He ruined it. Cut it up, nailed holes in it. Just... totally screwed it up."

Ally pressed her fingers to her lips in shock. Tyler glanced up at her, his expression tortured.

"What I don't get, what I will never get is *why*. What did I ever do to him to make him hate me so much? What did I ever do or say to earn that kind of treatment?"

It was a child's plea, issued from a man's mouth. Ally's chest ached for all the years of doubt and hurt he'd endured. This time she didn't resist the urge to go to him. She sat on the arm of his chair and slid both arms around him, pressing her cheek against the top of his head.

He remained locked in his rigid posture, unable to accept her comfort, but she didn't let him go. She couldn't.

"What did he say when you confronted him?" she asked quietly.

Tyler's shoulders lifted as he took a deep breath. "He blanked me. He said he'd never hit us, then he claimed we were out of control and he'd had to discipline us. Then he told me I didn't know what a knock was and that he loved us."

He dropped his head, fighting the emotion washing over him. The muscles beneath her hands felt as though they were carved from granite.

She'd seen him like this once before, hunched over the steering wheel of his truck. She held him more tightly.

"It's okay, Tyler," she whispered. "It's okay to be upset."

She could feel the resistance in him. Then, suddenly, he broke, turning toward her with a fierce neediness, his arms coming around her. His body shuddered and she felt the rough, choppy gusts of his breathing as he sobbed against her chest.

She splayed her hands over his back, holding him close, keeping him safe while he let out years of grief.

He made an inarticulate sound, his arms holding her so tightly it was almost painful. She smoothed her hand over his head and didn't let go.

Tears pricked her eyes but she blinked them away. Tyler did not need or want her pity.

As his breathing slowed and finally normalized, tension crept into his body in small degrees. She guessed what he was thinking, how much he must be regretting his moment of weakness. She knew without asking that he rarely, if ever, talked about his relationship with his father. That what had passed between Tyler and her was a rarity, that she was incredibly privileged to be trusted with his closely guarded truths.

She felt the honor keenly, as well as an aching

awareness that she was not what this man needed in his life. Not with her track record with personal relationships. And yet he was here, and she was holding him and now that she knew his full measure, now that she understood, she could no longer ignore the urging of her own heart.

She'd tried. She'd kept him at a distance and told herself she was doing the right thing, that it was for the best that nothing happen between them. But he'd come to her and he needed her and it was beyond her to deny him.

His arms tensed and she let him put some space between them. He used his forearm to wipe the tears from his face, not looking at her. "Sorry about that."

"Why?"

He glanced at her briefly. "I didn't come over here to dump on you, believe it or not."

She could see him pulling himself in more with every word, putting his armor on.

She dropped to her knees in front of him and caught both his hands in hers, forcing him to look at her.

"You think I pity you because of what you told me? You think that I think less of you because you cried?"

"I was wound up. I probably should have gone to the pub and gotten shit-faced."

He was so strong, so used to simply soldiering on. He couldn't conceive of a place where he could be safe. Where he could put down his burdens for a few hours and allow himself to feel and to grieve.

She acted on pure instinct, reaching out to cup his jaw in both hands, rising up to bring her face to his. She kissed him, pouring all her admiration and liking and lust into the contact, determined to prove to him that his revelations did not make him less of a man in her eyes.

After a long moment, he pulled away and she let him go.

"I don't want your pity, Ally." He sounded almost angry.

"Why did you come here tonight?"

It took him a moment to answer, and when he did he was deliberately offhand. "I don't know. I needed to get out of the house."

She shook her head, refusing to let him retreat. "You said yourself you could have gone to the pub. Or you could have left, gone back to Melbourne. You have friends there, I know. You could have done a million other things. But you came to me."

He stared at her, his gaze intent. She stared back, unflinching.

"That's why I kissed you, Tyler. For the same reason you came to me."

His gaze dropped to her mouth. "You said you weren't interested."

"I did say that." She offered him the ghost of a smile. "You should probably know that I don't have the greatest track record when it comes to making decisions in my personal life."

"Ally, I need…" He shook his head, unable to articulate what he needed, what he wanted. Why he'd come to her.

"I know. That's what I need, too."

Even though it scared the living daylights out of her.

She leaned forward and kissed him again and this time his mouth opened beneath hers and his arms encircled her. His kiss was demanding, consuming, undeniable. Which was fine with her, because she didn't want to deny him. Not anymore. She wanted to hold him close, for him to be a part of her body. She wanted to love and comfort and soothe him.

She made an approving noise and clutched at his shoulders, her fingers digging into the warm flesh of his back. Tyler answered by intensifying the kiss, scooping her body closer so that she was positioned between his open thighs, her breasts pressed against his chest.

The kiss deepened, grew more fiery. Hands began to rove, sliding beneath T-shirts, gliding over skin. Ally groaned as his hands found her breasts, his thumbs teasing her nipples. Tyler started drawing her tank top up her torso, muttering something against her lips.

"Sorry?" she said.

"I need to see you," he said, and she lifted her arms obediently as he tugged her top over her head.

His gaze fell on her breasts, hot and needy. She reached behind herself to undo the clasp on her bra. Her bra loosened, then slid down her arms. Tyler's gaze swept from one breast to the other, then his hands slid up to cup her bare flesh.

"Beautiful," he said, his voice low with desire.

She tugged at his T-shirt. "Fair's fair."

He had it off in seconds, and the next thing she knew she was on her back on the rug, Tyler on top of her. His chest was hot and hard against her breasts, the press of skin on skin satisfying and arousing all at once. She could feel his erection against her belly, could feel how ready he was, and she instinctively parted her thighs. He came to rest between them, his hard-on pressing against her through the soft fabric of her yoga pants. She shifted her hips restlessly, increasing the pressure, then he lowered his head and took a nipple into his mouth and she arched away from the floor, moaning low in her throat as sensation shot through her body.

Her fingers wove into the thickness of his hair and gripped tightly, holding him in place as he licked and sucked and tongued her breasts. She shivered, desire building on desire until the craving to have him inside her overcame every other consideration.

"Take your jeans off," she panted, reaching for the stud at his waist.

She worked it free, only to find more buttons. She groaned with frustration and tugged the buttons free from the soft denim with impatient hands. She pushed his jeans and underwear down his hips and he lifted his hips obligingly, taking his weight on his elbows while he kicked off the pants. She pressed her palm flat against his chest, then slid it boldly down the plane of his chest and belly until she encountered the thick length of his erection. Her fingers wrapped around the velvety skin, stroking, learning the length and breadth of him.

Tyler swore under his breath, then she felt a tug at her waist as he rolled away from her and started peeling her yoga pants down her legs. Within seconds she was naked and he was on top of her again, his erection nudging at the slick wetness between her legs.

Her hands found his backside, urging him closer, but he resisted.

"Condom." He started to pull away, reaching for his jeans.

She shook her head, halting his retreat. "I'm on the Pill. And I trust you."

She wrapped her legs around his waist and thrust her hips forward in silent invitation. All hesitation was gone as he slid home in one long, wet glide. Ally gave a little whimper at how perfect and hot and hard he felt.

Even though she wanted—needed—him to move inside her, even though she could feel the quivering tension in him, he remained still, buried to the hilt. He kissed her, his tongue teasing hers, his lips demanding, his arms banding tightly around her as he marked the moment indelibly in both their memories.

The first time they became one. The first moment of intimate connection.

He broke the kiss, using his elbows to take his weight as he pulled back enough to look into her eyes. He framed her face with his hands, tracing her cheekbones with his thumbs as they lay chest to chest, belly to belly, hip to hip.

"Ally."

Only then did he start to move, setting up a slow, inexorable rhythm, inviting her to join in. And all the while he stared into her eyes.

She got lost in the myriad silvers and grays of his irises, lost in the thrust and withdrawal of his body and the crazy-making friction building between them.

It didn't take long for need to overwhelm everything else. There was too much fire, too much longing, too much emotion. She started to pant, clawing at Tyler's back, making inarticulate noises as her climax swept toward her. He lowered his head and pulled her nipple into his mouth, his other hand sliding between their bodies to find the damp curls at the juncture of her thighs.

She tensed as his thumb brushed over her. Her body clenched around him. Then he caressed her again and she came, his name on her lips, her body bowing off the rug.

He murmured encouragement near her ear, riding

out her orgasm, milking the last shudder from her. Then and only then did he give himself over to the moment, his thrusts becoming wilder, more urgent. She urged him on with her hands and her body. He thrust deeply one last time, then he pressed his cheek against hers and his breath came out in a heated rush as he climaxed.

For a brief moment he was deadweight on her as he relaxed against her. Then he stirred and started to roll to one side.

"Not yet. Stay with me," she said.

He stilled, looking into her face. "I'm not exactly a lightweight."

She smiled slightly. "I like it."

His eyebrows rose, but he didn't try to withdraw. He pressed his cheek to hers again, his weight settling on her. She flattened her palms against his back and smoothed her hands over him, mapping the breadth and strength of his shoulders, tracing the long, lean muscles either side of his spine, curving her fingers over the resilient roundness of his backside. The hair on the backs of his thighs was crisp and soft, the muscles there very firm, while the skin over his hips was as smooth as silk.

He was beautiful, inside and out. Masculine to the bone, with a big, finely hewn body, his outward strength matched only by his tender, generous soul.

She rested her hand in the center of his chest, feeling the thump-thump of his heart and the rush of his blood as his body cooled. She could smell their mingled sweat and the earthy scent of sex and, beneath that, the sunshine warmth of Tyler's skin.

"I'm an idiot," she said very quietly.

He turned his head to look at her. "How so?"

"If I hadn't been so stupid, we could have done this days ago."

"Ah."

She waited for him to say more but he didn't.

"That's all you have to say? *Ah?*"

"I'm being diplomatic."

He was smiling, his eyes warm, his body relaxed and loose.

She smoothed a lock of hair from his forehead, glad that, for the moment, the shadows were gone from his eyes. He deserved a little lightness, a little happiness after the darkness of his recent past.

"You know what would make this moment perfect?" she said.

"What?"

"Ice cream."

He laughed, then slowly the smile faded from his lips. "Ally Bishop. Where have you been all my life?"

She smoothed his hair again, her chest aching with emotions she wasn't even close to being ready to acknowledge. "Waiting."

Then she nudged him gently and he rolled to the side.

"Nuts About Chocolate or raspberry ripple or

both?" she asked, her tone deliberately light as she
pushed herself to her feet.

"Is that a trick question?"

She smiled and went to find the ice cream.

TYLER WOKE TO THE SCENT of vanilla and spice. A
warm body curled beside him on the bed, soft and
rounded in all the right places.

Ally.

They were spooned together, her back to his front,
his arm around her waist. He could feel the regular
rise and fall of her breathing, and for long minutes
he simply lay there, enjoying the intimacy of close
human contact, the comfort of skin on skin.

She'd saved his sanity tonight. He'd been half out
of his mind after the fight with his father. The urge
to follow his father into his room, to grab him by the
throat and force him to acknowledge his own brutal-
ity had been almost overwhelming. But Tyler had
never used violence to get his own way. So instead
he'd found himself on the street, his keys in hand,
thoughts of escaping to Melbourne and his home and
his life in his mind. He'd made it into the truck, put
his seat belt on—but he hadn't been able to make
himself start the engine.

He'd been utterly lost then. He couldn't go, he
couldn't stay. Somehow, he'd wound up on Ally's
doorstep. From the moment she'd opened the door,
her calm, ready acceptance had been like a balm.
She'd simply waited and the words had come.

It was the first time he'd told anyone about his childhood. He wasn't sure what he'd expected, but she hadn't reeled in horror or broken down in tears or insisted on calling the police. She'd listened. She'd asked all the right questions. And when he'd lost it, she'd offered him the wordless comfort of her arms.

Humiliating to admit how much he'd needed it. He was a grown man, with a life of his own. All this stuff with his father had happened years ago. The old man should have no power over him anymore.

Yet Tyler hadn't been able to drive away.

That was the part that got him the most. The tears he could live with. Just. But for the life of him he couldn't understand why he felt compelled to stay, why, even now, lying in his lover's bed, a part of him worried that his father was in the house alone when he wasn't fully recovered from his operation.

Because Tyler was weak? Because his father still had some kind of hold over him? What kind of man took so much crap and still refused to walk away?

The tension had returned in his chest and belly. Ally stirred in her sleep and he realized he'd tightened his grip on her. Gently he eased away from her, rolling onto his back. One hand propped behind his head, he stared at the ceiling, trying to understand himself.

"Roll over and I'll rub your shoulders."

He turned his head to find Ally watching him, the

concern in her big brown eyes discernible even in the dim light.

"I didn't mean to wake you up."

"I can sleep anytime." She reached out and smoothed a hand over his chest. "It's not every day I offer ice cream *and* a free back rub. It's a pretty good deal."

He smiled faintly, catching her hand and lifting it to his mouth. He kissed her fingers. "Some other time, thanks."

He was way too wound up to relax into a massage, his brain churning.

"I know you're not big on talking, but sometimes it does help."

"Women always say that."

"Because it's true. Crying helps, too, but I know I'll never get you to concede on that one."

"No kidding."

She didn't say anything more, simply pressed her body alongside his and rested her head on his shoulder. There was nothing demanding or expectant about her silence—she was simply there, available and open. After a long few minutes Tyler took a deep breath.

"I wanted to go tonight. Wanted to get in my truck and drive and leave him to work it out for himself. But I couldn't. And I don't know why."

"Don't you?" Ally shifted so she could look him in the eye. "Do you want me to tell you?"

When he didn't say anything, she reached out and

ran a finger along the stubble on his jaw, her touch light. "Because you couldn't drive off and leave an old, sick man on his own. That's why."

He knew it was true, but he didn't like it. "I should be able to. After everything he's done. He deserves worse. He deserves to die alone."

"I'm sure he does. But you're not like him." Her eyes were depthless, soft as velvet. "You're a loving, compassionate man, Tyler Adamson. It's a miracle, given what he did to you, but you are. You're a good, good man."

There was so much warmth and emotion in her gaze. Tyler looked away, uncomfortable. Growing up, being hard had been the only value worth aspiring to, both to withstand his father's attacks and to prove to himself that he wasn't a victim. As a grown man, he'd prided himself on needing nothing and nobody and solving his own problems, righting his own wrongs.

"You think being compassionate is a sign of weakness, don't you?" Ally asked.

He shrugged noncommittally. Ally might not be a trained psychologist, but she was bloody good at putting her finger on the heart of things at times.

She pressed a kiss to his mouth. "It takes great courage and strength of character to be generous when you have every reason to be otherwise. You're the strongest man I know, Tyler. I wish I was half as strong."

He traced the delicate arch of one of her eyebrows.

What she was saying was flattering but it went against every lesson of his life. She turned her face into his hand and kissed his palm.

"I know there's nothing I can say to convince you. But I hope you believe me one day."

Because he didn't know how to respond, Tyler rolled toward her and slid a hand up her belly toward her breasts. She made a small, pleased sound as he cupped the warm weight of her in his hand.

She had a very sexy body, soft and curvy, full-breasted. Her skin was smooth and clear, her nipples a pale pink, like the blush inside a seashell. He circled them with his thumbs, watching as they hardened to arousal.

"You're setting a dangerous precedent here, you realize. Twice in one night," she said.

He smiled. Then he set himself to the task of proving to her exactly how dangerous he could be.

CHAPTER EIGHT

ALLY WOKE AT EIGHT TO find the bed empty beside her. She blinked, then a slow smile spread across her face as she remembered last night.

Tyler, making love to her. Insatiable. Intense. Gorgeous.

Then she remembered the catalyst for their encounter and her smile faded. Last night had been… incredible, but it hadn't changed the world. Bob was still next door, and he still needed care. Tyler's ordeal was far from over.

The difference, though, was that she knew now, and the days of keeping her distance were over. She would do whatever she could to ease Tyler's burden. Whatever it took.

A footfall in the hallway drew her head around. Tyler appeared in the doorway with a glass of juice and a plate of toast. She blinked in surprise. She'd assumed he'd gone next door.

"I didn't know whether you'd prefer jam or peanut butter, so I did a piece with each." He was wearing nothing except his boxer briefs and she tried not to stare too obviously.

Last night, she'd been too busy ripping his clothes

off to truly appreciate how beautifully he was put together. Now, her gaze ran over his square shoulders, well-defined pectoral muscles, flat belly and narrow hips. His thighs were muscular without being ridiculous, his calves a triumph of proportion. He was easily the sexiest, most masculine man she'd ever been with.

She swallowed a lump of pure lust.

"I like both. But you didn't have to make me breakfast."

"I was hungry. It seemed a little rude to pig out solo." He sat on the bed and passed her the juice.

She straightened and took a big mouthful. "What are your plans for the day?"

His gaze dropped to her breasts for a gratifyingly rapt second before he selected a piece of toast. "I need to check on Dad. And I promised Gabby I would get these designs to her by the end of the day."

"You can work here, if you'd like. I know you find it hard to concentrate over there." She took another gulp of juice. "And if you need me to, I'll sit with your father while you drive to Melbourne this afternoon."

He gave her a searching look and she knew he'd detected the effort she'd had to make to keep her tone neutral when she'd mentioned his father.

She reached for his hand. "He's not simply the nice old man next door for me anymore. To be frank, I'd be happy to never see him again. Or to have a chance to give him a piece of my mind. But I know that both those things put a burden on you. So I'll keep going next door and doing what I can to help. Whatever you want. But I want you to know I'm doing it for you, not for him."

She knew that for some people, Bob's illness and advanced years would be automatic grounds for a get-out-of-jail-free card for past behavior, but not for her. Tyler hadn't said much about his mother, but she understood that he'd had precious few people on his side in his lifetime. Well, Ally was on his side, and she was fiercely determined that he knew it and that all her comfort and understanding were for him. He deserved to have one champion in his life, one person who put him above anybody and everybody else.

Perhaps if Bob had sought to reconcile with Tyler in some way, she would feel differently. But he hadn't. Instead, he'd attempted to blame Tyler and twist the truth.

She couldn't see Tyler's face properly, but the grip on her hand tightened until it was almost painful.

"So do you want to work here today?" she asked again.

"If you don't mind."

"Well, I'll be honest, you're something of a distraction. But I'll suck it up."

His gaze fell to her breasts again. "I'm the distraction?"

She loved the heat in his eyes, loved the way he made her feel sexy and beautiful and desirable.

"Looks like it's going to be a long day," she said mischievously.

They showered together after they finished breakfast, then Tyler went to check on his father. Ally stood at the kitchen window, watching the house next door anxiously after he'd left. She wished there was some way she could take this burden away from him, some way she could protect him from whatever remaining ugliness his father had left in him. But even if she could, Tyler would never allow her to do so.

He climbed the fence an hour later and she went onto the deck to greet him. He had his roll of blueprints under his arm and a grim expression on his face.

"How'd it go?"

"Fine. He's alive and kicking. On his high horse, too. Told me he wanted an apology."

Ally blinked. "Wow. That's some serious denial he's got going on there."

The tightness had returned to his posture again. She grabbed his hand and laced her fingers through his and pulled him into the house.

"I've set you up in the study."

He stopped in the doorway when they arrived, surveying the empty desk and the bulletin board she'd cleared behind it.

"I thought you could hang some of your stuff up there so you could reference it easily. And I know the desk isn't as big as one of those big drawing boards you probably use, but I figure it's better than nothing."

"It's great, Ally. Perfect. But where are you going to work? I don't want to displace you."

"All I need is a chair and a pad and pen most of the time. The desk is pretty much wasted on me."

He hooked an arm around her neck and drew her close. "Thanks." He kissed her, his gaze warm and gentle.

"It was my pleasure."

And it had been. She'd enjoyed doing something for him. Something to make his life easier.

She eased out from under his arm.

"You've got work to do. And I need to start thinking about my next column."

"If you say so."

She turned for the door, only to start a little when a large hand bussed her on the butt. She gave him a dark look over her shoulder.

"That is so not going to become a habit."

"I've been wanting to do that from the moment I met you."

She stared at him, arrested. "Really?"

"You want a sworn affidavit? Or some other kind of proof?" He reached for her again.

She dodged out of the way, laughing, relieved to see him smiling again.

"Do some work. Then maybe we can talk about this proof thing."

They worked in separate rooms until lunchtime.

She made sandwiches for three and went with Tyler when he delivered one to his father. Bob was surly and taciturn and she stood in the doorway and watched as Tyler bit his tongue and didn't rise to any of his father's baits.

Amazing how differently a person's behavior could appear when viewed through a new prism. She'd always been mildly amused by Bob's gruff abruptness, but now all she could hear was the frustrated anger beneath his words. Her blood ran cold as she imagined him raising a hand to two small boys.

Bob caught her staring at him and she held his eye for a long, steady beat. She wasn't going to pretend that she didn't know what he was.

He was the first to look away.

She joined Tyler in the study when they returned to Wendy's house, curling up in the armchair with her latest letter file. It was nearly three when Tyler sat back in his chair, rubbed his neck and announced that he was done. Then he stood and plucked her file from her hands and kissed her, hard. They wound up mostly naked on the study floor, their lovemaking fierce and urgent.

Afterward, Ally watched as he dressed and rolled up his plans.

"I'll be back later tonight."

There was an unspoken question in his gaze. He wanted to know if he should come over. If she wanted him to stay the night again.

A wiser woman would say no. Things were already so intense between them.

"I'll be awake."

His slow, sweet, sexy smile was her reward. "I'll bring more ice cream."

She waved him off from the porch and then went inside. The bed was a rumpled mess so she changed the sheets. Then she sat on the freshly made bed and forced herself to face what she was doing—starting something up with Tyler Adamson, despite her promise to herself to never, ever let anyone down again.

She clenched her hands on her knees, her body tense. She didn't want to hurt him. Now, more than ever. He deserved happiness. He deserved every good thing life could throw at him.

Then, don't screw it up.

A great idea, but easier said than done. At least, it was in her experience. But it was too late to play it safe—it wasn't as though she could turn back time and change things so that she'd remained on the couch last night instead of wrapping Tyler in her arms. And she wouldn't want to, anyway, even if she could—last night had been one of the most challenging, precious, moving experiences of her life.

She stood and smoothed the quilt.

There was no point mooching around, agonizing over what might happen. After all, she'd been angsting and second-guessing herself since the moment she met Tyler and it hadn't stopped the inevitable from happening. So maybe the answer was simply to hand herself over to fate and take things one moment at a time and not get ahead of herself.

It wasn't exactly a plan, but it was *something*. And it would have to suffice.

AT SIX O'CLOCK, SHE GIRDED her loins and went next door. Bob was watching his game shows and he barely grunted when she let herself inside and said hello.

A far cry from his usual bright-eyed greeting. But he wasn't about to waste his charms on her now that Tyler had so clearly taken her into his confidence.

"Have you had your dinner yet, Bob?" she shouted over the din of the television.

When he didn't answer her, she stepped in front of the set and repeated her question.

He frowned at her and she could see him trying to work out how much rudeness he could get away with. "There's nothing to eat."

Ally knew for a fact that Tyler had prepared a plate of cold chicken and salad for his father's dinner, leaving it in the fridge. Leaving Bob to his show, she went into the kitchen to check the fridge. Sure enough, the meal was gone. On a hunch, she checked the garbage. The chicken and salad had been scraped, untouched, into the pail.

It was such a childish, spiteful act. Had Bob imagined he was making more work for Tyler? Forcing his son to do double labor in order to feed him? Punishing him in some way, as he'd punished Tyler as a child?

She stood in the doorway of the living room, watching him, trying to decide how to handle the situation.

A tuft of white hair sat up on his scalp, and the shirt he was wearing badly needed ironing. His hands moved restlessly on the arms of the chair and she was reminded of those long minutes she'd spent sitting beside him in the grass the morning he'd collapsed, holding his hand and willing him to live while she waited for the ambulance to come.

She'd felt so deeply for him then, lamented his aloneness so much. But he'd brought it on himself, and now that his son was here, helping him despite their troubled history, Bob still pushed him away and punished him.

Was he so unreachable? So set in his ways and bloody-minded that even now, when his days were numbered, he couldn't find it in himself to regret the past and try to make amends? One word, one look, of acknowledgment would mean so much to Tyler, she knew. It might even give him the closure he was so desperately looking for. It might even set him free.

The thought gave her impetus to move into the room and into Bob's line of vision.

"Bob. Can you turn the television down for a minute?"

He frowned, but he jabbed at the remote control

and the TV was muted, reduced to a flickering, distracting display in the background.

"I take it you didn't want the chicken?" she asked.

"It was off. Smelled funny."

She debated whether to call him on the lie, then decided to let it slide. She sat on the chair nearest to him and looked at him steadily.

"Is this the way you want things to be, Bob? Do you really want to spend your final days at war with your own son?"

"I don't know what lies he's been telling you, but he and his brother were always ungrateful little bastards."

"I believe him, Bob. I believe every word."

Bob's lip curled. "Think I don't know what you two are up to next door? Don't go thinking that letting him into your pants is going to get you anywhere, either. He's never been good at sticking at anything."

Ally thought of Tyler's thriving business and the way he'd put his life on hold to tend to his dying parent. She'd never met a more determined, honorable man in her life.

She stood. "Do you know what the saddest thing is? You have an incredible son. He's smart and he's kind and he's funny. And you will never, ever know him, because you're too small-minded and angry to see past your own failings. And they are your failings, Bob. Good men do not beat their children. No exceptions, no excuses."

She left the room before she said something she'd regret. Something irretrievable that would make it impossible for her to help Tyler care for Bob. She made him a sandwich, then she returned to the living room where the television was once again blaring.

She grabbed the small side table from the corner and dragged it until it was beside Bob's chair, placing the plate on it.

"If you throw this out, you'll have to make your own dinner or go hungry," she said.

Bob didn't acknowledge her. She returned to the kitchen and tidied up. Standing at the sink, her gaze fell on the shed. She turned off the tap and dried her hands and headed for the door.

There was still enough daylight left for her to open the doors and find the light switch on the inside wall. She stepped over a box of old tap fittings and the shaft of a broken trimmer and stopped in front of Tyler's table.

As he'd reported, Bob had all but destroyed it. The once-smooth wood was hacked and scarred, the delicate inlay shattered in parts, missing in others. There was one small section where the marquetry had escaped unscathed and she ran her fingers over it, feeling the smooth fineness of the work, marveling at the beauty Tyler had created.

She knew next to nothing about cabinetmaking, but she knew he'd spent hours on this table. Days. She imagined him working on it, young and eager to show his parents what he'd achieved, how far he'd come. Imagined the quiet pride he must have felt when he gave it to his mother.

A sudden conviction came over her. She gripped the edges of the table and lifted it, stepping over the boxes of junk and carrying the table out of the shed. She put it down so she could turn off the light and secure the door, then she carried the table to Wendy's house. She set it down in the living room and examined it again. The damage seemed even more profound now that it was contrasted with Wendy's delicate antique furniture.

It didn't matter. The important thing was that this was Tyler's table, and now it was safe.

"RIGHT. WE ALL SORTED?" Tyler said, shutting his diary with a snap and standing.

It was past seven, and he and Gabby had finally said goodbye to their client. The meeting had lasted almost an hour longer than he'd anticipated, but the upside was that the rush hour traffic out of the city would have cleared by the time he hit the road.

He started tossing things into his briefcase, only looking up when he registered that Gabby hadn't responded.

She was watching him, eyes narrowed, lips pursed. "What's going on?"

"What do you mean?" He slid a spare set of mechanical pencils into his briefcase.

"Why are you so keen on getting out of here? Anyone would think the building was on fire."

"Don't even joke about it."

"Seriously. What's going on? I gather from what you haven't said about your father that things have been pretty heavy going on that front?"

"Yeah. Well. Can't teach an old dog new tricks. He's determined to be an ass, and I'm determined to stick it out, so we're locked in this thing till it's over."

"You know, that's the most you've ever said about your father in all the years I've known you."

Tyler frowned. Had he really been so tight-lipped? "Probably because I hadn't seen him for ten years. He wasn't exactly at the top of my mind."

Although he'd always been there in some way.

"It's more than that. You seem…different. Lighter."

He gave her a look. "Lighter? What does that mean?"

"I'll give you an example. In the meeting just now, when that interior designer said she wanted to go with the beech on the bedside tables even though it isn't traditional, you didn't even bat an eyelid. Normally you would have gnashed your teeth and argued in favor of the cherry. But you simply made a note of it and moved on."

"She's the customer. And I've got better things to do with my time."

Gabby pointed a finger at him. "Exactly. Since

when did you have better things do to with your time than defend your designs?"

He stared at her. She stared back. Finally he shrugged.

"I've met someone."

Gabby's face lit up. "Really?"

"Yeah. Her name's Ally. She lives next door to my father."

"And you two are...you know?" Gabby made a gesture with the fingers of both hands.

"Very ladylike. You've been hanging around with the guys too long."

"I'm going to take that as a yes. Tell me about her." Gabby propped her butt on the edge of his desk.

"What do you want to know?"

"Whatever you've got. You're one of my favorite people in all the world, and I want to know who this woman is who's made you so happy."

Tyler had been about to tell her to mind her own business, but her words arrested him.

"And maybe I want to pick up a few tips for next time around. Since she seems to have succeeded where I failed."

Tyler considered her a moment, trying to read her. She'd been the one to break off their relationship, and in the two years since there had never been a hint that she still had feelings for him. But there had been a look on her face just now...

"It was a joke, Tyler." She rolled her eyes. "Get

over yourself. Now, are you going to tell me about her or not?"

"She's in her early thirties. Short. Dark hair. She writes the Dear Gertrude column in the paper."

"I love that column! Gertrude rocks."

"Ally does, too." He thought about what she'd said to him this morning.

"Oh, boy."

"What?"

"You are toast. Utterly gone. Besotted."

He shook his head.

"Don't bother denying it. You are smitten beyond the point of no return," Gabby said. "When can I meet her?"

"I don't know," he said, remembering Ally's reluctance to enter into anything with him and her insistence that she would be leaving in a few weeks time *no matter what.* "It's complicated."

"Complicated how?"

"You're a very nosey person, you know that?"

"I'm a concerned friend with a vested interest."

He sighed. There was a reason he avoided these kinds of conversations.

"Okay," Gabby said. "I'll back off. But if you like this woman as much as I think you do, you need to make sure you're both on the same page."

"Yes, Mom."

Gabby slid off his desk. "Careful, or I'll come up with a reason to delay you leaving."

"You seem to be forgetting something—I'm the boss."

She made a rude noise. "When in doubt, appeal to authority. A classic loser's move."

He grabbed his briefcase and the roll of designs and headed for the door. He tapped her on the head with the roll as he passed by. "One day that mouth of yours is going to get you in trouble."

He left her to lock up, but her words stayed with him as he drove to Woodend. Last night and today had been great, working with Ally, sharing lunch with her, making love on the study floor. Knowing he had her in his corner had made all the difference in dealing with his father. He hadn't felt so pressured, so cornered. So alone.

But there was no escaping the fact that Ally had resisted his first attempts to do something about the chemistry between them. And she'd been very clear that she had no plans to hang around once her current stint of house-sitting was up.

He'd never been the kind of man who got carried away with his lovers. There had always been a small, essential part of himself that he'd held back. But with Ally…he'd given her everything. Revealed his darkest, most vulnerable places.

His gut told him that last night had changed things for both of them, but his head wanted to nail her down, wanted to hear the words of confirmation come out of her mouth.

Too bad for his head, because he was never going

to initiate that conversation. Not only because that wasn't his style, but Ally was far too skittish, far too reluctant a recruit to their relationship for him to start asking those kinds of questions.

He would simply have to wait and hope and trust his gut.

ALLY WAS IN BED, READING the latest edition of *House and Garden* magazine when she heard Tyler's footsteps on the porch. She slid from the sheets and opened the door wearing only her tank top and a pair of panties. Tyler stilled, his gaze sliding down her body. Then he passed her a small cooler.

"You might want to put that in the freezer before I jump you."

She gasped out a laugh, but he wasn't kidding, sweeping in the door and pulling her into his arms. Her knees went weak as he kissed her with a hungry intensity.

"I missed you," he said when he finally came up for air. "And you should always dress like this. Always."

"Let me put the ice cream away," she said, slightly breathless.

"Move fast."

She found him sitting on the edge of the bed when she returned, his shirt off but his jeans still on, flicking through her *House and Garden* magazine.

"You running low on entertainment?" he asked, one eyebrow raised.

"No." She reached for the magazine.

He gave her a curious look and tweaked it out of her reach. "Is this yours?"

"Yes."

"It's *House and Garden*."

"So?"

He looked bemused. "You live out of a suitcase. You're a gypsy."

"It doesn't mean I can't read glossy magazines. I like the pretty pictures."

She yanked the magazine from his hand and slid it under the bed, tugging the skirt into place. When she turned around, Tyler was crowding her. She thought he was moving in to kiss her. Instead he dropped to one knee and lifted the skirt of the bed.

"*Tyler.* Have you ever heard of privacy?"

He ignored her, sliding a stack of glossy magazines out from beneath the bed.

"*Vogue Living, Belle Maison, House Beautiful*— flown in from the U.S., no less. *Better Homes and Gardens, Elle Decor, Country Living...*" A quizzical smile played on his lips.

Ally crossed her arms over her breasts. "What?"

"This is a bit of a dirty little secret, isn't it?"

"They're magazines. I told you, I like the glossy pictures. I find them relaxing."

"They're *home decorating* magazines. Full of glossy pictures of other people's homes."

She used the side of her foot to shove the stack

back where she'd had it. "I don't see what the big fuss is."

"You don't think there's any irony in a woman who scoffs at possessions and has no home of her own being addicted to homemaker magazines?"

Ally pressed her lips together, feeling more than a little exposed. "It's not an addiction," she muttered.

"How many do you read a month?"

She shrugged.

"Five? Ten? Twenty?" he asked.

"I don't know. Most of them come to me on subscription. I never really keep track."

"You subscribe?" He laughed incredulously.

"I really don't see what's so amusing."

She tried to march from the room but he hooked an arm around her waist and swung her toward the bed. She landed on her back and Tyler was on top of her in seconds. She tried to wrestle her way out from under him, but he just grinned down at her.

"Why are you so upset?"

"I'm not!" She heard the echo of her own strident tone and winced. She forced herself to meet his eyes. "They're just magazines."

"Okay. If you say so." But he looked very pleased about something.

Before she could question him, he ducked his head and used his teeth to pull her tank top down. When he'd exposed her left breast, he kissed his way back up the curve and pulled her nipple into his mouth.

"Did I mention that I missed you?" he said as he switched to her right breast.

After they'd messed up her nice clean sheets, she donned a robe and went to scoop some of their favorite treat.

"I meant to say, good choice on the flavors," she called.

He'd stopped at Trampoline and bought tubs of Peanut Nutter and Violet Rumble, the second being very high on her list of favorites thanks to its chunks of crunchy sponge toffee.

"I remember you saying you liked the Peanut Nutter," he said from close behind her and she nearly jumped out of her skin.

"You need a bell, like Mr. Whiskers."

"Any suggestions on where I should hang it?" He slid his arms around her waist.

"I have a few ideas."

She fed him a spoonful of ice cream over her shoulder, then concentrated on filling their bowls. He let her go so she could lead him into the living room to eat on the couch. He stopped in his tracks when he entered the room.

"I hope you don't mind, but I rescued it," she said.

He frowned, walking closer to the table. She watched as he rubbed the scarred rim with his thumb.

"I was thinking that maybe you could repair it."

She couldn't get a read on him, couldn't tell if he was upset or annoyed or grateful.

"It'd take a miracle."

She joined him beside the table. "But you could do it, couldn't you? You could make it beautiful again."

He hesitated a moment, then he put down his bowl and bent so that his eyes were on a level with the surface. He moved around the table, inspecting it closely, running his hands over the various gouges and pits. Then he crouched lower and ran his hands up and down the legs. Finally he stood and collected his ice cream. "I could do it."

"Do you want to?"

His gaze returned to the table for a beat. "Yeah. Yeah, I think I do."

She slid her arm around his waist.

"Thanks for rescuing it for me."

There was so much warmth in his eyes, it scared her. He was watching her closely, so she forced a smile.

"Better eat, it's melting." She focused on her own bowl, and after a few seconds he did the same.

Moment by moment, remember?

She joined Tyler on the couch, feeling the warmth of his body alongside hers as she sank into the cushions. He smiled at her, a little distracted, and she knew he was thinking about how he was going to fix the table. Pushing her doubts away, she rested her head on his shoulder and dug into her dessert.

This, right now, was a great moment, and she was determined to enjoy it.

THE FOLLOWING DAY, TYLER waited until Ally filed her column at midday before telling her to put on her swimsuit.

"Why?"

"There's a place on the river I want to check out. Jon and I used to go there as kids. I thought we could take a picnic."

"A picnic sounds nice."

"That's the general idea. I figured you deserved a break."

"Me? You're the one with the double workload."

"But he's my father."

She frowned but didn't say anything. He followed her to the bedroom and watched as she flipped open her suitcase.

He'd noticed before that while she'd unpacked most of her clothes, she kept a few things in the case still, things she didn't need every day. As though she was prepared to leave at the drop of a hat and wanted to ensure she had a head start on packing.

"I didn't even know there was a river around here," she said as she rummaged.

He tapped the side of his nose. "Local boy. Secret knowledge."

"So, local boy, is this a bikini kind of place or a one-piece kind of place?"

"Definitely bikini," he said without hesitation.

She gave him a dry look.

He put on his best innocent face. "What?"

"I'm not sure you're the best person to take advice from on this subject."

"With my hand on my heart, no one is going to notice what you wear except me. And I've always been a bikini man."

"I bet you have."

He was already wearing a black tank top and a pair of old jeans he'd hacked off at the knees and he leaned his shoulder against the door frame as Ally pulled a bright aqua suit from her suitcase.

"You want me to help you on with that?" he asked, pushing away from the door frame and taking a step toward her.

She laughed. "Anyone would think you hadn't gotten lucky this morning."

"It's your fault for being so sexy."

She made a face at his compliment and he closed the remaining distance between them to take her into his arms.

"You don't think you're sexy?"

"Marilyn Monroe was sexy. Monica Bellucci is sexy. I'm...cute. At best."

"You're sexy. Trust me."

He kissed her, and when things started to get interesting, she slipped from his grasp.

"We're never going to get out of this room if you don't leave me alone to change."

Tyler thought of the plans he'd made. If he had

his way, he'd consign them all to hell, but he wanted to give Ally a treat. She'd given so much to him and his father, and he wanted to give her something in return.

"I'll check on Dad," he said reluctantly.

She waved him off with a cheeky grin. The age-old tension crept into his neck and shoulders as he walked the short distance next door. Two days on from their argument, his father was still punishing him, refusing to answer his questions, behaving like a spoiled child. It reminded Tyler of the heavy silences they'd endured as children, tiptoeing around his father's moods. Frankly, Tyler wondered where his father found the energy—Tyler had never been able to sustain a bad mood for longer than a few hours. His father, however, had turned the sulk into an art form.

The house was blessedly quiet for once as he entered, the television switched off. He found his father at the kitchen table, frowning over a crossword puzzle. He looked up briefly when Tyler entered, then returned his attention to the puzzle without saying a word.

"Ally and I are heading out, but there are sandwiches for your lunch in the fridge," Tyler said.

His father ignored him. Tyler stared at him for a beat, then he crossed to the counter and wrote down his phone number. Tearing the sheet off, he dug around in the junk drawer until he found some tape and stuck the note to the side of the phone.

"Call me if you need anything, okay?"

Again, no response.

In reality, his father was so recovered from his operation that he really didn't need anyone making meals for him and supervising his showers any longer. This morning the nurse had taken Tyler aside and told him that she didn't think it was necessary for her to visit on a daily basis anymore. Between the two of them they'd decided to reduce her visits to weekly check-ups for the time being. If things changed—or, more accurately, *when* they changed—she would increase her visits again.

Essentially, they were in a holding pattern, waiting for the cancer to make the next move.

Tyler wondered how his father was dealing with this calm before the storm. If they had a different kind of relationship, he'd try to talk to him about it. But they didn't. All the same, one day soon they were going to have to sit down and talk about some things. What arrangements, if any, his father wanted made. Who he wanted to perform the service.

Not a conversation Tyler was looking forward to, on several fronts.

"I'll see you later, Dad."

When his father continued to ignore him, he headed for the door. Ally was trying to stuff two bulky beach towels into a too-small bag when he returned.

"Here, let me take care of that," he said.

She handed the towels and bag over. "This ought to be good."

He slung the bag onto the bed and draped both towels around his neck.

"I could have done that," Ally said, chagrined.

"So why didn't you?"

She poked her tongue out at him. He grabbed her by the shoulders and turned her toward the door.

"Stop trying to distract me."

"I was trying to insult you, actually."

"You're going to have to try harder. And use a different body part."

He urged her forward but she dug her heels in.

"Wait, I need sunscreen. And we should take something to drink. And what about lunch?"

"All taken care of."

"Huh."

She allowed him to usher her into his truck, and he headed into town. He stopped to collect the picnic lunch he'd ordered from the local café, then he took the freeway north until he found the turnoff he was looking for. The truck began to rock and buck as they drove onto a deeply rutted unmade roadway.

"Good grief. Where are you taking me?" she said, clinging to the armrest.

"I told you, it's a secret place."

"No kidding."

The road became increasingly rough as they neared their destination. Finally he spotted the distinctive crowns of a line of willow trees ahead and the truck entered a small clearing. He parked in the shade in deference to the hot midday sun.

"I feel like I'm in *Deliverance*," Ally said, peering through the windshield suspiciously. "Any second now we'll hear the sound of banjo music."

He got out of the truck and collected the picnic basket. "Come on, smart-ass."

She followed him up a short, well-worn dirt track, making cracks about *Deliverance* all the way. Then they emerged on the riverbank and he watched the teasing expression fade from her face as she took in the gently sloping grassy bank and the clear water of the river, all framed by swaying weeping willows, their long branches dipping in and out of the water with the breeze.

"Oh, wow. This is beautiful."

It was, although it was smaller than he'd remembered, the trees bigger, but he figured that was only natural, since it had been twenty years since he'd last been here.

"Jon and I used to hang out here every summer when we were young. All the local kids did, before they built the pool in town. There used to be an old tire swing, and we'd practice our Tarzan moves hanging out over the water."

"There still is, look." Ally pointed to the nearest willow.

It took him a moment to spot the tire propped in the fork of the two main branches. Someone had obviously stowed it out of sight for safekeeping. He put down the picnic basket and crossed to the tree. On close inspection, he discovered the tire was still firmly tied to one of the large overhead branches with a thick length of rope. He tugged the tire free and let it drop so that it swung like a pendulum.

"I've always wanted to try a rope swing. They make them look like so much fun on all those soft drink ads," Ally said, her voice muffled.

He turned to find she'd laid the towels out on the grass and was pulling off her tank top, stripping down to her bikini top and khaki hiking shorts. He watched as she bent over the picnic basket, enjoying the way her breasts pressed forward, creamy smooth and round.

"Yum. There's pasta salad. And fruit salad for dessert," she said, glancing at him.

She shook her head when she realized what he'd been staring at.

"Food first," she warned him.

He shrugged as though there had never been another thought in his head and joined her on the towels. They grazed on the selection of deli meats and salads, polishing it off with vanilla ice cream and fruit salad and a crisp, cool apple cider to wash it all down. Ally rolled onto her back afterward and closed her eyes.

"That was delicious." She cracked an eye to look at him. "This place was worth the bumpy ride, by the way."

He lay down beside her and she wriggled closer

so that she could rest her head on his shoulder, his arm around her. Tyler gazed at the blue sky, her head a heavy weight near his heart. The only sound was the rush of the river. His belly was full, and he had an incredible, generous, smart, funny woman lying next to him. He could feel the warmth of her body alongside his, could smell her unique scent.

All the things he wanted to ask her, all the things he wanted to know faded into the background. Time slowed. The world shrank.

"This is really nice," she said drowsily.

"Yeah. It is."

The kind of nice a man could get used to, he decided as he drifted toward sleep.

If he was given half a chance.

CHAPTER NINE

HE WASN'T SURE HOW LONG he dozed for, but when Tyler woke Ally was gone. He sat up and looked around, only relaxing when he saw that she was near the big willow, investigating the rope swing. He watched with growing amusement as she attempted to climb onto it, only to fail repeatedly as it rocked beneath her weight and tipped her off.

"It's a two-man job," he called.

"Then what are you waiting for?"

He stood and stretched, then walked down the slope to join her.

"Give me a boost," she said, her eyes bright with anticipation.

"First, the golden rule of river swings. Gotta check the water depth before you do anything."

He walked to the edge, stripping off his tank top. Tossing it onto the grass, he waded into the water. The river bed was soft beneath his feet, the water icy cold despite the heat of the day. He waded in up to his waist, then up to his chest. He turned back to face the bank, the current tugging at him gently.

"See where I'm standing? This is where you want to jump off, okay? Water's nice and deep."

"Okay."

He made his way back to where she waited.

"Up you get." He grabbed the rope and steadied the tire.

"Hang on a minute."

She shed her shorts, tossing them toward his tank top. She gave him an excited smile, then placed her hand on his shoulder for balance while she stepped into the hole of the tire, then climbed on top, sliding her legs either side of the rope. She gripped the rope with both hands and looked at him expectantly.

"Okay. I'm ready."

"One last thing."

He leaned forward and kissed her. She tasted like sunshine and fresh air, her mouth hot against his. She made one of the small, approving noises that drove him crazy and he angled his head to taste more of her. He tried to move closer, but the tire was a big, round impediment to greater intimacy. Ally started to giggle, finally breaking their kiss to laugh out loud.

"So much for the tire swing as a sex aid," she said.

"Yeah. I won't be rushing to the patent office with that one."

She looked so adorable that he couldn't resist dropping one last kiss onto her nose. Then he stepped away and got a good grip on the tire.

"Hold on."

He walked backward, pulling Ally with him, his

arm and leg muscles straining as he took more and
more of her weight. Then he let go and shoved with
all his might. She let out a whoop of delight as she
swung out over the river.

"Get ready to jump!"

Ally shifted on the swing, but when the critical
point came, she hesitated. "What if I fall on my
face?"

"Then you fall on your face. It's part of the fun."

The tire reached its farthest point and started to
swing toward shore.

"Now! Go now!" Tyler called.

But again she didn't let go. And she was coming
in, fast.

Tyler glanced over his shoulder. The tree trunk
was directly in her path. He'd pushed Ally with so
much momentum there was a good chance she'd hit
it before the tire ran out of steam.

Bracing himself, he stepped into the path of the
tire.

"Tyler. Get out of the way!" Ally called as she
swooped toward him.

"It's me or the tree, babe."

The swing twisted as it approached and she hit
him back-first with a hard slap of skin on skin.

"I've got you," he said.

His arms wrapped around her body but the tire's
momentum pushed him off his feet and knocked the
air from his lungs. He waited for the impact of the tree
trunk, but the swing petered out inches shy of making

contact then began a more leisurely sway toward the river. He planted his feet firmly and brought the tire to a jerking halt. Ally twisted frantically to look at him.

"Tyler. Are you all right? My God. You haven't broken anything, have you?"

She was so comically concerned he couldn't help but laugh.

"I'm fine. But you need some serious coaching on tire swinging."

She scrunched her face in self-disgust. "I know. I'm a big chicken. Once I got out there, I kind of froze."

"Let me show you how it's done."

He helped her slide off, then he pulled the tire toward the tree as far as he could. He leaped onto the tire and pushed off with one smooth motion, swinging out over the river with one foot braced in the center of the tire, the other on the top. At the farthest point of the arc, he let go and performed a perfect water bomb into the middle of the river. Cold water splashed over him, rushing up his nose and covering his head.

"That was so cool. I want to learn how to do that," Ally shouted from the bank when he broke the surface.

He pushed his hair off his forehead and wiped the water off his face with his hands. "I'm sure we can work something out."

He waded toward shore, deliberately choosing to

exit where the bank was steepest. He pretended to struggle, watching Ally surreptitiously. As he'd anticipated, she immediately rushed forward to offer him her hand.

"Here," she said, bracing her legs to take his weight as she leaned toward him.

He wrapped his hand around her forearm, then he looked straight into her eyes, not even trying to hide his grin. "Too easy, Ally."

Her eyes widened with shocked understanding as he jerked her into the water. She splashed in up to her thighs, her body tensing as she registered the temperature of the water.

"Oh! It's cold!" she gasped as the water splashed her torso. "You sneak, let me go."

"Come for a swim first," he said, pulling her deeper into the water.

"It's too cold."

The water was up to her breasts now.

"No, it isn't. Not once you get used to it." He tugged her arm one last time, pulling her close and wrapping both arms around her. Her skin was warm against his in the cool water, her nipples pebbled and hard against his chest.

"How old are you? Fifteen?" she asked, but she was smiling and she closed her eyes and relaxed into his body when he kissed her.

He slid his hands to her backside, cupping her round little derriere and lifting her against him. She sucked on his tongue and pressed closer, her arms wrapped tightly around his neck.

After a few torturous moments, he broke their kiss. His heart was thundering in his ears and he was painfully hard. Any desire he'd had to swim had been well and truly superseded by another, more urgent need.

"Put your legs around my hips."

She complied readily and he got a good grip on her backside before he started walking toward the bank.

"Tyler! You'll give yourself a hernia. Put me down, I'm too heavy."

"You're small enough to fit in my pocket. Lighter than thistledown."

All the same, he was straining a little by the time he reached the towels.

"Still lighter than thistledown, am I?"

"Got you where I wanted you, didn't I?"

He tumbled her onto the towels and rolled on top of her. Her nipples were still hard from the cold water and he tugged her bikini top to one side as he lowered his head toward her. She caught his ears before he could pull her nipple into his mouth.

"Tyler. Anybody could see us." She sounded like a scandalized Sunday-school teacher.

"But they won't. We'd hear a car coming long before it got here."

He slipped free of her grasp, lowering his head and

circling her nipple with his tongue before pulling it into his mouth.

She gripped his shoulders. "Tyler." It was a half-hearted protest.

"Think of it as the ultimate form of getting back to nature."

While she was pondering that, he tugged her bikini top off and switched his attention to her other breast.

It wasn't long before Ally was fumbling at the wet waistband of his jeans, trying to gain access to his erection. The wet denim fought him every step of the way as he tugged it over his hips. When he hooked a finger into the waistband of Ally's bikini bottoms, she bit her lip and glanced up the slope toward the trail.

"Trust me. This is more private than your back-yard," he said.

She lifted her hips and he pulled her bikini bottoms down. He surveyed her, all pink and cream in the dappled light, her dark curls beckoning enticingly.

"You look good enough to eat. Strawberries and cream."

She gave a muffled protest as he started to kiss his way down her belly. He pushed her legs wide with a gentle hand, caressing her inner thigh soothingly.

"Relax. Count to ten," he said with a half-smile. "It'll be over before you know it."

She remained tense until he lowered his head and took the first long, slow taste of her. Quickly she turned to liquid in his hands, moaning and quivering and digging her fingers into his hair and shoulders until he slid up her body again and plunged deep inside her.

Her head dropped back and she closed her eyes as he started to move, her breath coming in choppy little pants. He caressed her breasts and her hips and the smooth skin of her belly, loving how soft and warm and womanly she was. Loving the feel of her around him, beneath him.

She came silently, her breath catching in her throat, her hands clutching at his backside. He let himself go, too, riding her shudders to his own completion, looking into her eyes as she dazedly came back to earth.

He rolled away afterward, breathing heavily. Ally lay languid and supine beside him for a full twenty seconds before she remembered where she was and scrambled to pull one of the towels over both of them.

"You realize we broke about ten different decency laws, don't you?"

"I counted eleven. But you might be right."

"You're a bad influence, Tyler Adamson."

"That's what my mother used to say."

She fell silent for a moment, then propped her chin on her hand. "You never talk about your mother," she said.

He could hear the unspoken questions in her voice. "Neither do you."

He had some questions, too.

"That's different."

"Is it?"

"If you don't want to talk about her, it's okay."

"I'm fine talking about my mother, but there's not much to tell, to be honest. She wasn't a very happy woman. Her and Dad used to fight a lot, especially when we were younger. She was stuck at home with two little kids all day, and he'd stay at the pub after work. I think she resented the isolation. Resented us."

He waved a fly away with his hand.

"She never did anything to stop him hitting you?"

"Never. She used to tell us it was our fault, that if we were good boys Dad would never have to lay a finger on us."

"Did he ever hit her?"

He shook his head. "They'd just go at each other verbally. One of the clearest memories of my childhood is my mother crying at the kitchen table. It was practically a nightly event."

Ally pressed a kiss to his shoulder, resting her cheek against him for a long moment in wordless sympathy.

"What about your mom?"

She stared at him as though she didn't know where to begin.

"You told me the other day she was an artist," he prompted.

"That's right."

"What sort? Painter, sculptor?"

"Painter. She worked mostly with acrylics. I guess you'd say her style was post-modernist."

"Would I know any of her work?"

"Probably not. She had a bit of success in the early seventies, but mostly she relied on friends or boyfriends to give her somewhere to live and help her get by."

"Pretty precarious way to live." Especially with a child in tow.

"Yes, but she was very charming and she never outstayed her welcome. She was always flitting around. New York, Paris, London, Sydney, Spain. She even lived in Rio for a while. She was the ultimate free spirit, really, and I think it's safe to say I was the unplanned mistake of her life."

She gave him a dry look.

"My aunt told me once that my mother was devastated when she found out she was pregnant, especially since it was far too late to do anything about it. Very typical of my mother, not even noticing she was pregnant until it was staring her in the face."

"What about your father?"

"Never knew him. Don't even know his name." She shrugged as though it made no difference to her.

She sat up and reached for her bikini bottoms, shuddering as she pulled them up her legs. "Is there anything worse than putting on a wet swimsuit?"

Tyler could think of worse things. Like being told you were a mistake, for instance, and never knowing your own father.

"I take it your mom stopped traveling when she had you?"

"She tried. But she couldn't handle it. She hated being tied down, hated 'sublurbia,' as she called it. So she left me with my grandmother when I was about six months old."

She grabbed for her bikini top and put it on.

"I don't remember Gran very much, although I always feel as though I should. She died when I was five."

"What happened then?"

"My mother came back for me and I started traveling with her."

Ally sank to the ground beside him, lying on her belly while she plucked at the grass.

"So you were an international jetsetter at five?"

"For a while. I didn't like it very much. I used to freak out at all the different places we stayed in. Sent my mother crazy." She laughed, shaking her head. "There was this one place in New York, a big old apartment in SoHo or somewhere. It took up a whole floor, but it was completely empty, utterly desolate, except for the bedroom where we stayed. I used to have nightmares about all those dark, empty rooms and wake up screaming. Then there was the place in Provence, with the scary outdoor toilet. More nightmares. And so on. Finally my mother talked her sister into looking after me."

She plucked a couple of bluebells from amongst the grass and started braiding their stems together.

"How old were you then?"

She screwed up her face, thinking. "I don't know. Six? Maybe seven. I don't remember exactly, but I hated being left behind. With a passion. Which probably explains why Aunt Phyllis was more than happy to hand me back to my mother when I was nine. I don't think I was a very grateful niece."

She shot him an amused look, inviting him to laugh at the misbehavior of her juvenile self.

"Doesn't sound as though anyone cut you much slack," Tyler said carefully.

Maybe he was misinterpreting Ally's words, putting a too-dark slant on them, but the childhood she was describing sounded far from ideal, being shunted from pillar to post, palmed off from mother to grandmother to aunt.

"Well, my mother was too self-interested to cut anyone but herself any slack. And Aunt Phyllis did her best with what she had. Which wasn't a lot, because I'm pretty sure my mother didn't send child support payments from whichever villa or loft or atelier she was crashing in."

She smoothed her thumb back and forth over the braid she'd made.

"It was better the second time around, though. I made friends with the houses we stayed in the moment we arrived, so the nightmares weren't a problem anymore."

"How do you make friends with a house?"

"It's very simple. You do a tour, and you find the door that groans and the window that rattles and the stair that creaks. Then, on the first night, when you're lying in bed and the house starts making its nightly settling noises, you tell yourself 'that's the window in the second bedroom' or 'that's the third stair from the bottom' or whatever. Works a treat. Comes in handy when you're house-sitting, too. I can get the lowdown on a new place in half an hour these days, no problems."

Her tone was light, her expression untroubled, but Tyler felt a stab of empathy for a little girl who'd been so afraid of being left behind again that she'd forced herself to stare down her fear in order to overcome it.

"How did your mother die?"

Ally's expression became sad. "She was staying at a friend's place in Spain. They were renovating, and some of the electrical work wasn't up to standard. There was a fire. The coroner said she'd been drinking, which was probably why she didn't make it out."

"How long ago was this?"

"Ten years this June. I was backpacking in America when I got the news."

She was quiet for a moment, then she threw the

bluebell braid into the long grass and pushed herself to her feet.

"Enough sad stories. Come on, rudey-nudey man, you promised you were going to teach me to jump off the tire swing properly."

She tossed him his cutoff jeans, then started across the grass toward the tire swing.

He stared after her, still processing everything she'd told him, trying to reconcile what he'd learned with what he already knew of her. He thought about the stash of home decorating magazines she had hidden under her bed and the advice column she wrote and her inexhaustible supply of pajamas. Then he remembered the way she'd warned him that first night he'd kissed her. *I'm a girl who leaves,* she'd said.

"Are you coming or not?" she called, squinting her eyes against the sun.

Tyler rose and wrapped one of the towels around his waist.

"Try and stop me," he said.

Then he went to teach Ally how to jump.

THE NEXT TWO WEEKS SLIPPED through Ally's fingers like water. Apart from three occasions when Tyler had to return to town to take care of business matters, he slept in her bed by night and worked in her study by day, occasionally disappearing into Bob's shed to work on his table. Between the two of them they cared for his father, preparing his meals and cleaning the house. Bob held on to his sullen defensiveness for longer than she would have thought possible, but eventually they all settled into a routine of sorts and she found herself exploring a new kind of happiness and contentment with Tyler by her side.

He was a wonderful lover, selfless and sensual and insatiable. He was also a wonderful conversationalist—not chatty, by any means, because he would never be a garrulous man, but when he chose to say something, it was always smart and witty and to the point. He made her laugh a lot, and he made her think. Most of all, he made her feel complete, in a way she had never experienced before.

Quite simply, she felt as though she'd come home. Which was crazy since Tyler was only in Woodend for as long as his father needed him and she had no idea where she was going once Wendy reclaimed her home. Her life was as up in the air and temporary as it had ever been. And yet it had never felt more solid, more grounded.

Sitting in the living room on a sunny afternoon, Ally doodled on her notepad as she allowed herself to imagine what might happen next. She'd stuck staunchly to her live for the moment rule most of the time over the past weeks, but with Wendy due home soon she figured it would be smart to put some thought into her immediate future.

Normally she would have another house-sitting job lined up by now, but she hadn't so much as taken a second look at the two prospects she'd bookmarked at the beginning of the month. It felt wrong to think of moving on when Tyler still needed her.

She made a rude noise at her self-deception. She was so pitiful, so terrified of what was happening between them that she couldn't even admit it to herself.

Grow a set, Bishop.

She took a deep breath. Then she finally acknowledged the truth to herself: she'd fallen in love with Tyler. And she suspected—no, she knew, in her gut and in her heart—that he loved her, too. It had been the elephant in the room for the past week, the topic they danced around every time they lay in each other's arms or caught each other's hands when they walked down the street or simply made eye contact unexpectedly.

But she had a feeling the elephant's days were numbered. She sensed there was a conversation on the horizon—and she had no idea how she was going to handle it when it finally arrived, what she was going to say if Tyler said the things she thought he was going to say and asked the things she thought he would.

Panic tightened her chest as her mind ran over the options open to her—stay or go. She wasn't sure which terrified her more.

She heard the sound of the front door opening and put down her pad and pen, very deliberately pushing the whole mess to the back of her mind. Wendy wasn't due for two more weeks, after all. There was no reason for her to start manning the lifeboats prematurely.

"Couldn't stay away, huh?" she called down the hall.

Tyler had disappeared next door after lunch and told her not to expect him until dinnertime, a pretty common occurrence the past few days as work intensified on the table.

She waited for him to respond, but he didn't. Curious, she went in search of him. She found him in the bedroom, his back to the door as he bent over something. He was wearing his cutoff jeans again, and she spared an appreciative glance for the way the worn denim showcased his backside and thighs.

"Thought I wasn't going to see you until dinner?"

"Yeah. I finished early." He straightened, turning to face her. Then he took a step to one side and she saw what his body had been shielding.

He'd finished the table. She took a step forward.

"When...?"

"A few days ago. But it takes a few passes to get the polish right."

She reached out a hand but stopped short of touching it. The finish was too perfect, too fine.

"Tyler. It's *stunning*."

And it was. He'd replaced the ruined marquetry with a new design, a many-pointed star made up of a myriad of red-hued woods. The top tapered to a simple bevel on the rim, and he'd honed the legs and reeded them, making the table appear more delicate and refined.

"It's okay, you can touch it. It's meant to be used," he said, an amused glint in his eyes.

She ran her fingers over the central star, unsurprised to find it silky smooth beneath her hands.

"I didn't know there were so many different shades of red."

He moved closer. "This is Jarrah, and that's redgum. And this is red cedar. There's a lot of variation within each species, but I had some good off-cuts at the workshop to play with."

"Tyler, it's beautiful."

"I'm glad you like it, because it's yours."

She stilled, her gaze flying to his face. He was watching her carefully, a small, slightly nervous smile on his lips.

"You're giving this to me?" she asked, her voice rising to an incredulous squeak.

"I'd like you to have it. If you'd like it."

She lay her hand on the table. She couldn't believe he was serious. "Are you nuts? I'd love to have something so beautiful. It's…God, it's breathtaking. I don't know what to say."

She could see he was pleased that she liked his gift. She looked at him, her chest aching with emotion.

"Tyler." But she couldn't find the words to express what she was feeling and she shook her head, angry with herself for being so inarticulate.

The doorbell sounded. Ally frowned.

"I'll get it," Tyler said.

She caught his arm as he brushed past her. "Tyler. It's beautiful. I love it. I'll cherish it forever," she said.

For God's sake, say it. Tell him you love him. Tell him you're crazy about him.

But the words got caught in her throat and wouldn't come out. Tyler gazed into her eyes for a moment, then he leaned close and kissed her briefly on the mouth.

"I'm glad."

He left the room. She stared after him for a beat, angry with herself for choking.

You're a chicken, Bishop. A big old yellow-belly.

It was absolutely true.

She surveyed the table again. She hadn't owned a piece of furniture for nearly four years, and she'd never, ever owned something this precious. All her stuff had always been cheap and disposable, designed to be temporary. This piece was an heirloom. A small, perfect masterpiece that should be enjoyed for generations.

She could hear Tyler talking to whoever was at the front door. She registered that the other voice was vaguely familiar. She listened for a moment and realized it sounded like Belinda, Bob's nurse.

A trickle of unease ran down her spine. She stepped into the hall. Tyler was standing on the front porch, his face creased with concern as Belinda talked. He seemed to sense her presence and he glanced at her. She knew immediately that something was wrong and she hastened to join him.

"What's happened?"

"Nothing drastic," Belinda said. "I was just explaining to Tyler that I've noticed Bob's been using more of his painkillers lately. So I had a little chat with him, and he's been experiencing back pain."

They'd been waiting for this, so it wasn't exactly a shock. But it was still grim news.

"I think we should get him into hospital for some tests, so we know what we're dealing with and how best to make him comfortable," Belinda said.

"When?" Tyler asked.

"I can make a call now, see what's available. Tomorrow, if possible."

Tyler nodded. "If you wouldn't mind."

"That's what I'm here for."

They waited while Belinda moved off to make her call, watching the other woman pace the sidewalk as she talked and listened. Ally squeezed Tyler's hand.

"You okay?"

He shrugged. "Had to happen, right?"

"Doesn't make it any easier."

"No."

Belinda ended her call and rejoined them on the porch.

"9:30 a.m. tomorrow."

"Great. Thanks for that, we appreciate it," Tyler said.

They ate dinner with Bob that night, enduring the blare of the television to keep him company. Not that he'd requested it—he would prefer to cut his tongue out, Ally suspected—but it felt like the right thing to do.

She watched Bob eat his meal, thinking about all the things he'd denied himself with his refusal to engage with his son.

But Bob's journey wasn't over yet.

She sent a little prayer out into the universe that Bob would find a moment of truth and clarity to offer his son before it was too late. For Tyler's sake, if not his own.

THE NEXT DAY, SHE WAITED with Tyler while Bob was scanned and his blood was taken, then she waited some more when Tyler and Bob met with the oncologist to hear the results of the tests.

Tyler's expression was flat, utterly unreadable as they exited the consultant's rooms. Bob kept his gaze on the floor, but she could see he was fighting to control himself.

Later, after they'd driven home and settled Bob in his armchair with his puzzle books, she and Tyler sat on the deck next door and he told her that the doctor had confirmed that Bob's cancer had spread.

"Soon his liver function is going to drop. And then it's going to be pretty fast, the doctor said."

Ally blinked away tears. "Has Bob said anything?"

Tyler shook his head. "You know what he's like."

"Yeah, I do."

Tyler sighed. "I need to call Jon, let him know what's going on."

"Sure."

He went into the house. Her gaze moved over the fence. What must Bob be feeling right now? Was he scared? Relieved? Resigned? Angry?

She drew her knees into her chest and rested her cheek on her knees.

Over the past weeks she had found an uneasy middle ground within herself where Bob was concerned. She would never feel the same warm affection for him that she once had—she couldn't, not when she knew what he'd done to Tyler—but the initial burning outrage she'd felt had been tempered by the sheer mundanity of caring for him. It went against her nature to deny someone in need. It was as simple as that. Despite his many, many failings and cruelties, she had it in her to feel pity for Bob.

Tyler exited the house and sat beside her. She looked at him in silent question and he nodded.

"He's coming. Catching the first flight out tomorrow. I'll drive into the city and pick him up."

"When was the last time you saw him?"

"I don't know. Eight years, maybe nine."

"What's he like?"

Tyler thought for a minute. "You know, I really have no idea."

"Maybe you two can get something out of this after all."

"Maybe."

She poked him with her finger. "Don't go all silent and manly on me. This is important. You two got through your childhood by battening down the hatches and enduring. I get that, but things are different now. Take it from someone who has no one, a brother is a precious thing."

Tyler looked at her, then he reached for her hand. "You don't have no one, Ally. You have me."

Such simple words, but they made her chest expand with warmth and love.

This man. This incredible, loving man.

She reached out to cup his face, but once again the words in her heart failed to make it out of her mouth. To cover the moment, she leaned forward and pressed a kiss to his lips, holding him close, trying to tell him with her body what she wasn't able to verbalize yet.

Soon, she told him silently, deepening the kiss. *Soon.*

Following his lead as he pulled her down onto the deck, she tried to ignore the little flutter of apprehension in the pit of her stomach.

TYLER GOT UP EARLY TWO days later to make the drive into the city to pick up his brother. Ally stirred briefly when he got out of bed, then again when he dropped a kiss on her cheek on the way out the door.

"Drive carefully," she murmured before burrowing into the pillow.

He stared at her for a moment, thinking about the conversation that was looming between them. Wendy was coming home soon. Which meant it would be time for Ally to move on—if she wanted to. If she was prepared to walk away from what they'd built between them.

On a good day, he knew, absolutely that she would stay. Knew that she loved him, and that the intense connection he felt with her was a shared and mutual thing.

But there was always that half-packed suitcase in the corner to remind him that Ally had a long, long history of not putting down roots.

There's a first time for everything.

He bloody hoped so, anyway, because he loved her with everything he had, and he didn't want to even think about a future that didn't include her. A concession indeed from a man who'd once prided himself on needing no one and nothing.

He left the house quietly, pausing for a moment in the quiet of predawn. The forecast was for another hot day. The last time Tyler had checked, it had been below freezing in Toronto—Jon was in for a rude awakening.

He let himself into his father's house to check that all was well before he took off. He expected his father to be asleep, but when he ducked his head in the door of his father's bedroom he saw the bed was empty. The living room was empty, too, and the kitchen. He checked the toilet and bathroom, then headed out to the yard, only to pull up short when he spotted his father sitting at the bottom of the steps.

"Dad. You gave me a scare."

His father shifted his head slightly but didn't fully turn around. "You're up early."

"I'm going to pick up Jon. Remember?"

His father nodded. Tyler descended a few steps.

"Are you okay? You're not in pain?"

"Only so many tablets a man can take."

"We can talk to Belinda if you need more."

"I'm fine."

Tyler stared at the back of his father's head. Ally had given his hair a trim last week and his hairline was military straight. The lines on his neck were deeply scored, the skin loose with age.

"Dad. If there's anything you want to talk about, anything you want to say, now's the time," Tyler said quietly.

He waited, his body tense.

His father didn't say anything.

Well. It had been a long shot, anyway.

"I'll see you when I'm back with Jon."

He was about to slip back into the house when his father spoke.

"Don't put your foot down, those coppers are everywhere with their radar guns. Cost you a bomb if you get caught."

"I'll be careful."

His father grunted and Tyler walked through the house to the front door.

They were on the home stretch now, whether they liked it or not. All they could do now was hang on and endure.

ALLY WOKE AGAIN AT EIGHT and showered and made herself breakfast before she went next door to see if Bob needed anything. She could hear the television as she walked up the path. Bob had started early today. Usually he liked to do his crosswords in the morning and save the television for when his game shows started in the afternoon.

She rang the doorbell to let him know she was there, then let herself in the front door.

"It's only me, Bob."

There was no response, but that was hardly surprising, given the racket of the television.

She walked into the living room. Sure enough, Bob was in his usual chair, his crossword puzzle book on his knee.

"Good morning. Have you had breakfast yet or would you like me to make you some?"

When Bob didn't respond, she stepped into his line

of vision, which was when she saw that his glasses had slipped slightly down his face and that his eyes were closed.

"Bob."

She rushed forward, grabbing his hand to find his pulse. To her relief she felt the faint, weak flutter of Bob's heartbeat against her fingertips.

He was alive. But something was wrong. She checked his airways were clear, then went into the kitchen to call an ambulance. She gave the address and what information she had, then hung up and bit her lip. She thought about calling Tyler, then decided to wait until the ambulance arrived so she could give him more information. He would be at the airport by now, waiting for his brother's plane to land. There was nothing he could do from so far away.

Déjà vu swept over her as she knelt beside Bob's chair, holding his hand while she waited for the ambulance. It had barely been a month since she'd last done this. How the world had changed.

The ambulance arrived within five minutes and she stood to one side while the attendants checked Bob over. He remained unconscious and she felt a growing dread as they took his vital signs.

"He has cancer," she explained. "It's in his liver, kidneys… And he's on medication."

"Do you know what kind?" the female attendant asked.

Ally went to collect the bottles.

"What do you think is wrong?" she asked when she returned.

"Looks as though he's had a heart attack. Pretty big one, judging by his heart trace." The woman gave Ally a sympathetic look. "Might be a blessing, given what you told us."

"I need to make a call."

She moved into the kitchen, her hands icy as she dialed Tyler's number. She pressed her fingers against her closed eyelids, willing herself not to cry. They'd all known this was coming, that Bob was dying. As the woman had said, a heart attack was a blessing, given his circumstances.

The call connected.

"Tyler, it's Ally. You're not driving, are you?"

"I'm at international arrivals. Jon's flight has been delayed by half an hour. What's wrong?"

"Your father has had a heart attack. He's still alive, but the ambulance crew seem to think it's pretty serious."

There was a profound silence at the other end of the phone. She imagined Tyler in the middle of the busy airport, trying to think.

"Where are they taking him?" he finally asked.

"Kyneton again. I'll go with him."

"Thanks, Ally."

"I'll see you soon, okay? And I'll keep you updated."

Tyler said something, but the sound was muffled.

"Sorry, I missed that."

"I just saw Jon."

"Okay, I'll let you go. Be safe."

"I will."

He ended the call.

She returned to the living room as the attendants were strapping Bob into the stretcher.

"I need to grab my phone and purse from next door, then I'll come with you," she said.

A tense ambulance ride later, Bob was rushed into the emergency department. Ally was asked to wait in the waiting area and she wrapped her arms around herself and paced anxiously.

She didn't know what she was hoping for. It seemed cruel to will Bob to live simply so Tyler could say his final goodbye. As for Jon... She could only imagine how he was feeling right now.

"It's Ally, isn't it?"

She glanced up to see Bob's oncologist standing in the doorway of the waiting area.

"Yes, that's right. I'm Bob's neighbor."

"Tyler's not around?"

"He's picking up his brother from the airport."

"That's unfortunate. I don't suppose you know if he and his father ever discussed a D.N.R.?"

"I'm sorry, I don't know what that is," Ally said.

"Sorry—doctor speak. It's shorthand for Do Not Resuscitate. If something happens, we need to know whether Bob would want us to keep him alive."

God.

"I don't know. Tyler never mentioned it. Bob wasn't big on talking."

"I noticed. Last of the stoics."

"I'll call Tyler."

She pulled her phone out. The call had barely connected when it was picked up.

"Tyler's phone," a deep voice said.

For a moment Ally was thrown, then she realized it must be Jon.

"It's Ally. Is Tyler there?"

"He's driving."

"Jon, I'm sorry to do this, but can you ask him if he and Bob ever discussed a Do Not Resuscitate order? The doctor needs to know."

"Right."

She heard muffled conversation, then Jon came back on the line.

"Tyler says no."

Ally caught the oncologist's eye and shook her head.

"Can I talk to him?" the doctor asked.

"It's Jon, Tyler's brother," she explained.

Quickly she introduced the doctor before passing him the phone. A short, terse conversation later, the doctor handed back the phone, gave her a nod of thanks and left.

"Where are you?" Ally asked.

She'd overhead enough of the conversation to know what Tyler and his brother had told the doctor.

If Bob became critical, they'd agreed it was kindest to let him go.

"We're passing the turnoff for Macedon," Jon said.

Which meant they were only half an hour away.

"We'll see you soon." She slid her phone into her bag. She'd seen a coffee machine in the hallway. Something warm would be welcome right now.

She was taking her first sip when the oncologist returned. "Bob's awake, if you'd like to see him."

"Oh. Yes," she said, abandoning her cup on the nearest flat surface.

She followed the oncologist into the busy emergency department, stepping under his arm as he held back the curtains around one of the cubicles for her.

Bob lay flat on the bed, his bare chest covered with leads. Oxygen prongs pinched his nostrils and a monitor tracked his heart rate with audible beeps. She moved to his bedside and touched his arm and his eyes opened. It took him a moment to focus on her and she guessed they'd given him some sort of pain relief.

"Bob. It's Ally," she said.

Bob closed his eyes again. "Ally. You're a good girl," he said weakly.

She tried to think of something to say, something comforting that wouldn't require an outright lie.

"Tyler and Jon are on their way. They'll be here any minute."

Bob's hand moved on the bed. She reached for it and he gripped her fingers with surprising strength. He opened his eyes and looked at her.

"Don't want to die." He sounded frightened, like a child. Ally swallowed a lump of emotion. She didn't know what to say to him. They both knew he *was* dying. That if this wasn't the end, it was damn close to it.

She glanced surreptitiously at her watch, willing Tyler to arrive. Only ten minutes had passed since she'd ended the call, which meant they were still at least twenty minutes away.

"Thought the cancer would get me. But my bloody ticker gave out." He closed his eyes again and his grip slackened on her hand.

The monitor made a different sort of beep and Ally's gaze flashed to it. A series of uneven rhythms spiked on the screen. She glanced over her shoulder fearfully.

"Help! I think something's happening."

The curtain whipped back and two nurses and a doctor rushed in as Bob's monitor sounded an alarm.

"We need you to wait outside, please," one of the nurses said and Ally was suddenly on the other side of the barrier.

She stood there, arms wrapped around herself, listening to the hospital staff talking shorthand to one another for what felt like a long time. The alarm kept up a continuous whine.

Then, suddenly, there was silence.

Ally pressed her fingers to her mouth. A tear slid down her cheek. A few minutes later, one of the nurses slipped through the curtains.

"I'm sorry," she said simply.

Ally nodded, unable to speak for the moment.

"Would you like to sit with him?"

"Yes." Ally choked on the word.

It seemed wrong that Bob should be left on his own so soon. And Tyler and Jon would want to see him when they arrived.

"I need to make a call first," she said, her heart heavy.

"You'll have to go out to the waiting area to do that, I'm afraid."

Ally made her way out of the emergency department, pulling her phone from her bag. She found a quiet corner and dialed Tyler's number.

"Ally." It was Jon again.

She took a shuddering breath, forcing the words out. "I'm really sorry. Bob had another attack. He's gone."

A moment of silence. She could hear Tyler's brother breathing on the other end of the line.

"He's gone," Jon repeated, and she knew he was talking to Tyler and not to her.

The sound of fumbling, then Tyler's voice came down the line.

"Are you okay?" he asked.

She closed her eyes. Only Tyler could ask that five seconds after he'd learned his father had died.

"I'm fine. I'm so sorry."

"It's okay. We're ten minutes away. Hang in there, okay?"

She returned to Bob's cubicle to wait for his sons to arrive. They'd removed the prongs from his nose and the leads from his chest, and the heart monitor was now blank and silent. His arms were by his sides, resting on the bed.

Ally sat beside him and took one of his hands in hers and waited.

CHAPTER TEN

THE PICK-UP HAD BARELY stopped before Jon was out and racing across the parking lot toward the emergency entrance of the hospital. Tyler followed more slowly, understanding his brother's misplaced urgency. He, too, felt the need to make haste, in case there had been some kind of mistake, a last-minute reprieve.

There wouldn't be, of course. His father was dead. And it wasn't as though seeing him one last time would change anything. Everything that was ever going to be said between them had been said. Tyler knew that in his bones.

Jon had no such certainty, though. He'd flown halfway around the world and arrived twenty minutes too late. He hadn't said a word after Ally's phone call, but Tyler had felt the tension radiating off him in waves.

He'd been shocked by his brother's appearance when Jon had exited customs at the airport. His brother was unshaven, his eyes bloodshot. Understandable, perhaps, after a long flight, but he was also very lean, as though he'd lost a lot of weight recently. He looked like a man on the edge, a man in crisis.

Ally was hovering outside a closed cubicle when he arrived in the emergency department.

"Tyler," she said, opening her arms.

He walked into her embrace and held her close, inhaling the smell of her, feeling the warmth of her cheek against his own.

She sniffed and he pulled back a little so he could look into her face.

"You okay?" he asked.

"Stop asking me that. He's your father. How are you?"

He glanced toward the curtain. "I'm okay."

She studied him, a small frown pleating her forehead. "I'm so sorry you weren't here."

"It doesn't matter."

She frowned again but didn't say anything. He nodded toward the curtain.

"Is Jon in there?"

"Yes. I figured he'd probably want some privacy…"

Typical Ally, always thinking of others, always doing the right thing. He pressed a kiss to her forehead, then he released her and turned toward the cubicle.

"I'll wait here," Ally said.

Jon was standing near the head of the bed, arms crossed tightly over his chest, hands buried beneath his armpits. He was frowning fiercely as he stared at their father's body, his lips pressed into a tight, thin line as he fought to suppress strong emotion.

Tyler stopped beside him, taking in his father's stillness, the gray cast to his skin, the sunken boniness of his face. The cancer had stripped more weight from him in the past weeks, despite the fact that Tyler had been doing his best to provide hearty, nutritious meals.

Beside him, Jon made a choked sound.

"I know you probably had some things you wanted to say to him. Things you wanted to hear from him," Tyler said, carefully not looking at his brother. "If it's any consolation, even if we'd gotten here in time, he wouldn't have said anything. I don't think he could."

"He was an old prick. A sadist. He—" Jon used his forearm to take a swipe at his eyes.

"Mate." Tyler could feel his brother's anguish and fury, all the unresolved feelings clamoring for out. He laid a hand on his brother's shoulder.

Jon's face twisted as his emotions got the better of him, then he jerked away from Tyler's touch and pushed past him, disappearing through the curtain in a flurry of fabric.

Tyler let him go. He was willing to bet his brother had never cried in front of anyone in his life.

He returned his attention to the bed. A strand of his father's hair was sticking up and Tyler reached out to smooth it into place. He let his hand rest on his father's skull, aware that a few short weeks ago, the thought of touching his father with anything approaching gentleness would have been unimaginable to him. Proximity had burned out most of Tyler's anger, and Ally had done the rest. Her patience and understanding and love.

He studied his father's face one last time. For good or for ill, the man who had once lived in this body had been the biggest influence in his life. He'd shaped Tyler in a thousand different ways. He'd been cruel, violent, selfish. And he'd also been scared and small and isolated.

Not much of a life, when it came down to it.

"Rest in peace," he said quietly.

He turned away from the bed. There would be arrangements to make, papers to sign.

His father was dead. It was over. Finally.

SIX HOURS LATER, TYLER made the short walk from his father's house to Ally's. He and Jon had been busy making arrangements all afternoon. Ally had quietly bowed out after lunch, leaving the two of them to work through it together. He knew what she was doing: giving them room to become the kind of brothers she thought they could be.

It was a nice idea, but there was something closed off and hard about the man his brother had become. It would take a hell of a lot to break through all those barriers.

He could hear Ally clattering around in the kitchen when he entered.

"Hi," she called out. "I bought some beer. I figured you guys might need a drink."

Tyler stopped in the kitchen doorway. Ally was standing at the counter wearing her Shrek pajama pants tossing a salad, and he could see she'd made kebabs for dinner.

"Jon's not coming."

Her face creased with concern. "What's he going to do for dinner?"

"He'll probably get hammered and pass out."

"You Adamson men. Would it kill you to talk once in a while?"

"I talk."

"Sometimes."

He moved closer and hooked his finger into the waistband of her pajamas. "What do you want to talk about?" He tugged her closer.

She came willingly into his arms but her eyes were worried as she looked at him.

"I know you must be feeling cheated. You came here and put your life on hold so you could get some kind of closure with your father—and he died before you could clear the air."

Tyler caught her earlobe between his thumb and forefinger, caressing it lightly. She was so soft, every part of her warm and welcoming.

"We were never going to clear the air."

"I know he blanked you that time you fought, but I thought that once he'd had a chance to process the news he'd had this week that he'd change his mind."

He slid his hand around to the back of her neck, shaping his hand to her nape. "No."

"You sound so certain."

"I didn't get a chance to tell you, but I found him sitting on the back steps this morning before I left for the airport."

"Really? What was he doing?"

"Waiting for the sun to come up, maybe. I really don't know. But he was so quiet. It was the most reflective I've ever seen him. So I asked him if there was anything he wanted to say, anything he wanted to get off his chest."

"What did he say?"

"Nothing."

He watched understanding dawn in Ally's eyes. "God, he was such a stubborn old bastard."

"He was. Till the end."

She lay her head on his chest. He smoothed his hand over her hair.

"I hate that you didn't get what you needed from him."

"It's okay."

"No, it isn't. The least he owed you was acknowledgment. To look you in the eye and own his own actions."

"I know what happened. I don't need him to acknowledge it."

She lifted her head to look at him. "You're really okay with this?"

He thought about it for a moment. "Yeah, I am.

I came because I couldn't live with myself if I did anything else. I did my best by him. I can live with that."

Her gaze searched his face, then she stood on tip-toes and pressed a kiss to his lips. "You're a beautiful man, Tyler Adamson. I love you."

He stilled.

Finally—*finally*—she'd said it. He'd been waiting, taking his cues from her, biding his time. But she'd said it. At last.

"Does that mean you're not going to take off when Wendy comes back next weekend?"

There was a short pause before she answered. "I haven't got another house-sitting job lined up yet."

It wasn't really an answer, but he hadn't really asked the question he wanted to ask, either, had he?

"Ally. I love you. More than I ever thought it was possible to love anyone. Will you come to Melbourne with me, move into my place? Live with me?"

He heard her suck in a quick breath, but he knew his question wasn't a surprise. They'd been leading up to this since the moment they first met.

She gripped her hands together as though she was bracing herself for something. His gut tightened. He had no idea what he was going to say or do if she said no.

"Yes."

Relief made him stupid. He blinked. "Yes?"

"Yes."

He closed the distance that separated them and embraced her.

"God, I love you, Ally Bishop."

"I love you, too."

He kissed her. Despite the heaviness of the day, he felt a little giddy. She'd said yes. After all his caution, all his concern about stifling her and overwhelming her, she'd said yes.

"Let's go to bed," he said.

She glanced toward the counter. "What about dinner?"

"It can wait."

He waited while she stowed the salad in the fridge, then he pressed her against the wall and kissed her until she was pliant and breathless. They barely made it to the bedroom. He peppered her body with kisses, telling her he loved her, how much she meant to him. All the things he'd been holding inside for too long.

If today had taught him anything, it was the value of speaking and sharing and connecting.

Afterward, she dozed with her head on his chest. He stroked her arm, mentally making space for her in his closet, clearing out the spare room, rearranging the house so that she could make it her own.

Much easier to do that than to think about that small, telling moment when she'd clasped her hands together and braced herself before giving him her answer. As though she was forcing herself to the point.

He knew she had issues around settling. Hell, until he'd given her the table, she hadn't owned a single stick of furniture. She saw herself as a born nomad, a dyed-in-the-wool gypsy. But things were good between them. The past few weeks had proved that beyond a doubt. And she loved him. Surely that would be enough.

They would make it work. Somehow. He wasn't giving her up. Not when it had taken him thirty-seven years to find her.

TEN DAYS LATER, ALLY did one last quick survey of Wendy's house.

There was probably something she was forgetting. Normally when she house-sat she was very disciplined about where she left her things. This time, she'd gotten sloppy. She'd infiltrated every room of the house, and no doubt her friend would be finding traces of Ally's presence for months to come.

"I can't see anything obvious," she finally said.

Wendy looked up from where she was scratching Mr. Whiskers's belly.

"I can forward anything to you. Or come visit. I'm in Melbourne all the time."

Ally nodded. There was a tight feeling in her chest and she told herself she was simply being sentimental. A lot of good things had happened during the three months she'd lived here. It was only natural that she'd be sad about leaving.

Except the feeling in her chest didn't feel like sadness. It felt more like anxiety. Verging on panic.

Stop being such a drama queen. You want this. You love Tyler. There's nothing to freak out over.

She knew it was true, but she was still incredibly wary about moving into Tyler's home. When he'd asked her, she'd known that they'd reached a point of no return. The elephant had finally been named, and Tyler was asking her to make a decision about her future. Their future.

In all honesty, she'd expected it to be harder than it had been. But as she'd stood there looking at him, his declaration ringing in her ears, she'd tried to imagine life without him, all the mornings she'd have to wake up without him beside her if she stuck to the promise she'd made to herself five years ago and walked away.

It had been impossible. Literally unimaginable. So she'd said yes, and it had been both easier and harder than she'd thought. Easier, because she loved Tyler desperately, and harder because she'd immediately felt the burden of what she'd committed to.

It wasn't that she didn't want to live with Tyler. She did. More than anything she wanted to move in with him and started weaving the strands of her life with his. It was simply that she'd been here before. Not this exact same place, true—because she'd never felt as connected as she felt with Tyler—but close enough. She'd made promises. Put down roots. And then she'd started to get itchy feet and the walls had closed in and she'd had to get out of there—but not before she'd hurt someone. Daniel in London, Jacob in L.A., Bailey in Sydney.

It will be different this time. Tyler is different. He's the one. The man who will make staying in one spot doable. Bearable.

God, she hoped so. With every fiber of her being.

"I still can't believe Bob's gone. And so quickly," Wendy said, pushing herself to her feet. "I was away for only twelve weeks."

"The world can change in twelve weeks."

"I guess."

She'd notified Wendy about the funeral, and her friend had flown home to pay her last respects to her elderly neighbor. It had been a short service, and Ally had stood between Tyler and his brother at their father's graveside and grieved for both of them, as well as herself.

Bob had not been a perfect human being. In fact, he'd been a very flawed, angry, narrow-minded human being a lot of the time. But he'd produced two good men, and he'd not been without his small moments of humanity.

"You want a hand carrying your table out to the car?" Wendy was standing beside the table, admiring Tyler's craftsmanship again, the gleam of avarice in her eye.

Ally gave her a mock-steely look. "Hands off. I've already told you you can't have it."

"But it looks so good in my house."

"Then you'll have to commission one of your own."

"It wouldn't be the same as this."

Ally lay her hand on the table, thinking about all the work that had gone into it, the history behind it. "No, it wouldn't."

She let Wendy help her carry it outside, worried about bumping it against the door frame. They were about to descend the steps when a voice called out.

"I'll do that." Jon bounded up the path, ready to intervene.

"We can manage."

"All the same," Jon said. "I told Tyler I'd help you pack when he left yesterday."

Ally threw up her hands and stepped back. She'd already learned it was useless to argue with him. Tyler's brother had some very old-fashioned ideas where women were concerned.

She and Wendy watched as he picked up the table easily and strode down the path with it.

"Who would have thought there could be two in one family?" Wendy murmured out of the side of her mouth, her eyes glued to Jon's backside.

It was true—Jon was as good-looking as Tyler. They shared the same big build and dark hair, and they had the same square jaw. Jon's eyes were more gray than silver, however, darker and stormier, and his face more angular. He looked as though he'd lived a harder life than Tyler, too, the lines around his mouth etched deeply, his hair touched with gray at the temples.

"How long did he say he was hanging around for, clearing out the house?" Wendy asked.

Ally nudged her with an elbow. "It's open-ended. And you have a perfectly lovely boyfriend, remember?"

"I do, it's true. Which is probably just as well. Jon might be lovely to look at, but I have a feeling he'd be hell to house-train."

Ally studied Jon as he bent to the task of fitting the table into her already crowded car. Knowing what she did about Tyler and Jon's upbringing, she suspected he had more than his fair share of monkeys on his back.

"Yes. Some lucky woman's got her work cut out for her, that's for sure."

She returned inside to collect her handbag, then rejoined Wendy.

"Thanks for everything, Ally. It was a load off, knowing you were keeping the home fires burning," Wendy said. "Keep me posted, okay? I'm waiting for the next big announcement with baited breath."

Ally gave her a confused look and Wendy started humming the wedding march.

"No. We're not getting married," Ally said adamantly.

It was enough that she was moving in with Tyler. *More* than enough.

"Then maybe this, then." Wendy mimed a big

baby belly and held her back in the classic pose of pregnant women everywhere.

"No." Ally shook her head. She hoped her friend couldn't hear the thread of panic in her voice. "We're taking this one step at a time."

"Maybe you are, but Tyler's practically building nursery furniture and planning your retirement home. That man is crazy about you."

"I should get going," Ally said abruptly. "I want to make it to Tyler's place before it gets dark."

She kissed Wendy goodbye, then did the same with Jon, thanking him for his help. Then she slid behind the wheel, started the car and pulled away from the curb.

I can do this. I can move in with Tyler and love him and not make a mess of it. I can.

She gripped the wheel tightly and told herself the same thing over and over as she turned onto the freeway to Melbourne.

She knew she was making a mountain out of a molehill. Knew that the moment she saw Tyler again, all the doubts would fade. What they had together was right. The best thing that had ever happened to her. This time it was going to be different.

That's what Mom said with Tony, remember? Then she left him after nine months.

"It's not the same," she said out loud.

She heard her voice echo around the car and reached to punch on the stereo. She needed to stop thinking and simply let things happen. That's what she'd been doing all along with Tyler, and things had worked out fine. Just fine.

She got lost twice trying to find Tyler's house and finally had to pull over and call him for directions. He guided her the last few streets. When she turned the final corner, she saw him standing on the sidewalk, phone to his ear.

He was wearing his most raggedy, faded jeans and an old, worn T-shirt with a surfer logo on it, and he looked utterly precious and dear and familiar to her as she parked at the curb and cut the engine. Her heart gave a painful little squeeze and she practically fell out of the car, craving the reassurance and certainty she always felt when she was in his arms.

He met her halfway, scooping her into an embrace, and she kissed him with everything she had in her, holding him tightly, fiercely, her arms trembling with the force of her emotion.

He broke the kiss after a moment and laughed. "Miss me, babe?"

"Yes." She pressed her head against his chest, waiting for his steady presence to still the tumult inside her.

"How was the drive down?"

"Fine. No problems."

His hand caressed her back, but she could feel his distraction. He wanted to unpack the car and show her his home. Her home.

She let him pull away, even though every instinct told her not to let him go.

"You ready for this?" he asked, his eyes dancing with silver light.

"Of course."

He took her hand and she turned to face his house. It was exactly as she'd imagined—and also a million times better. A double-fronted Victorian, it had a central door with windows on either side. A bull-nose veranda shaded the front of the house. The smooth stucco finish on the facade had been painted a soft vintage white while the trim on the windows and veranda was glossy black. A neat box hedge lined the redbrick path, and the veranda was covered with earth-hued heritage tiles in a traditional tessellated pattern. A graceful bench sat to one side of the veranda, and matching cumquat trees were placed either side of the door in big stone pots. The lights were on in both the front rooms, giving the house an internal golden glow in the deepening dusk.

"It's lovely."

"Come inside."

She could see his pride, his excitement as he led her up the path and through the door. He wanted her to love his place as much as he did.

"Our bedroom is on the right, the guest on the left," he said as their footsteps echoed on the wide, worn planks of the floor in the generous hallway.

She stopped in the doorway of his bedroom—their bedroom—and looked at his big king-size bed and his beautiful wooden bed frame and nightstands. White plantation shutters were folded on either side of the front window and a dark chocolate-colored carpet covered the floor.

"I like your colors."

"We can change them if you like. None of it's set in stone."

"No, it's all lovely."

He gestured for her to explore further and she crossed the plush carpet and ducked her head into the doorway to the en suite. A gleaming antique washstand with a white marble counter and shiny chrome taps dominated the space. A freestanding claw-foot bath was situated in an alcove, a double shower next to it.

"Wow."

In a daze, she followed Tyler into the hall and beneath a decorative archway.

"This used to be the third bedroom," he said, throwing the door open.

She stared at the desk he'd set up in the corner and the cushioned window seat beneath the bow window. The walls were a buttery soft yellow, the trim a crisp white. The floor was covered with a faded antique rug in shades of umber, gold and brown. A carved bookshelf sat empty on one wall, waiting to be filled with books.

"I thought you could use this as your office."

He was watching her closely but for the life of her she couldn't think of anything to say.

The room was…perfect. From the color of the walls to the window seat with its fat, colorful cushions to the gleaming desk with its leather inlay. Just like a page in one of the magazines she spent hours poring over.

"I've always loved window seats."

She felt as though she'd fallen down the rabbit hole. She'd expected Tyler's house to be nice—the man was a meticulous craftsman, after all, and she'd already deduced that he was a bit of a neat freak—but this house was more than nice. It was mellow and worn in all the right places, it had charming quirks and modern finishes, and, most of all, it was filled with Tyler's warmth.

It wasn't simply a house, it was a home. A home with heart and warmth, a place to settle and be comfortable and put down roots.

She crossed to the desk, imagining herself working there, gazing out the window as she pondered an answer to one of her letters. She'd keep a big vase of fresh flowers in the corner at all times, and a fluffy throw blanket on the window seat in case she wanted to curl up with a book. And when Tyler was working from home, she could give him the desk to lay out his designs and she could write from the window seat…

"Come and see the kitchen."

It was as charming as the rest of the house—white country-style doors with wood countertops and an old-fashioned porcelain farmhouse sink. The living room boasted a huge fireplace and opened to a paved entertaining area and a stretch of grass bordered by trees.

"It's a bit bare out here," Tyler said, flicking on a light so she could see. "I'm not much of a gardener."

Ally shook her head, blown away. Utterly over-whelmed. "It's amazing. All of it. I feel as though I should ask you to pinch me."

Tyler smiled. "No pinching. Not yet, anyway."

He dropped a kiss onto her forehead. "I'm going to start unpacking your car before it gets too dark."

"Okay."

She followed him as he walked toward the front of the house, stopping in the doorway of the study again.

She was still standing there when Tyler returned with her table.

"You okay?"

"This is surreal," she said without thinking. "I feel as though I'm in a dream."

He frowned. "Is that a good thing or a bad thing?"

She forced a smile. "It's a good thing, of course."

He gestured toward the table. "In here or in the bedroom?"

"Um. Here, I guess."

He carried the table into the study and placed it near the window seat.

They made multiple trips to her car. She frowned as she realized how much she'd accumulated over the past few months. Normally it would take her only two trips to unpack her car, but somehow she'd collected a bunch of stuff while she was at Wendy's. For starters, she'd brought all her magazines with her, something she never did. Usually she donated them to a nearby women's shelter or left them for the owner of the house to enjoy. But not this time. She'd bought a few cookbooks, also another no-no, since books were hard to carry around. And somehow she'd bought more clothes than her suitcase could accommodate.

"I don't know how that happened," she murmured as Tyler lay the excess clothes on the bed.

"What?"

"I don't remember buying so many clothes."

"There's lots of storage, don't worry."

He crossed to the built-ins and opened the first set of doors.

"I've cleared out a space for you."

He left to collect the final items. She stared at the empty rails in front of her. She could see Tyler's clothes at the far end, pushed aside to make room for hers. She heard footsteps in the hall and Tyler appeared in the bedroom doorway.

"That's it, all done. I bought chicken for dinner. I'll put it on while you unpack."

"Sure. Great."

He disappeared. Ally turned to her suitcase, reaching for the zip to open it. The hand she stretched out was trembling violently. She stared at it for a moment—then she gave in to the panic battering at her from all sides and sank to her knees.

She pressed her forehead against the rough canvas of her suitcase, trying to get a grip on herself, trying to hold it together. She clenched her hands, pressed them tightly against her belly. Tried to breath through her nose, slowly and deeply.

Nothing helped. Everything in her still wanted to run screaming for the exit. Which was crazy. This place—this home—was beautiful and warm and welcoming. She could imagine herself cooking dinner in the kitchen, then lounging up on the couch with Tyler afterward, watching TV. She could imagine herself sleeping in on Sunday mornings, then getting muddy in the garden. God help her, she could even imagine little feet running up the corridor and the skitter of claws as the family pet followed their child.

And it was too much. Too big, too all encompassing. Too real. Too possible.

"Ally. What's wrong?"

Tyler's hand landed on her shoulder, warm and steady.

She shook her head, unable to articulate the realization crystallizing inside her.

"Ally. Talk to me. What's going on?" He tried to draw her into his arms but she stiffened and pushed him away.

"You're shaking."

"It'll pass. It's just a panic attack," she said.

He crouched beside her, his eyes dark with worry. "I didn't know you had panic attacks."

"I don't. Not full-scale ones like this. Not since I was a kid."

"Can I do anything?"

Ally stared at the carpet in front of her for a long moment. Then she slowly raised her head until she was looking him in the eyes. "You can let me go," she said.

There was a beat of silence before he responded. "You want to leave?" He sounded very calm. Almost as though he'd been expecting something like this.

"I can't stay."

"Are you sure about that?"

She held out her hand so he could see how much she was shaking. "A part of me wants this. But the other part of me knows it's not right. I told you from the start, I can't settle. Your house…your house is beautiful, Tyler. I want to believe I can live here with you and make it work, because I love you so much. But I can't even unpack my case."

"Right. The gypsy gene."

She started to cry. "I told you. I'm a screw-up. I've screwed up every relationship I've ever had. And now I'm going to mess things up with you and hurt you and I don't want to. I love you so much and I don't want to hurt you."

She started to sob, her body jerking with the power of her grief and misery. Tyler tried to pull her into his arms again but she resisted him.

"No. I don't deserve your comfort. I've led you on and made promises I can't keep. I tried so hard not to be like her, to keep my distance and not hurt anyone else, but I have. I have—" She broke off, unable to continue, curling in on herself.

Tyler pulled her into his arms despite her wordless protests, pressing her close and holding the back of her head in his hand as though she was incredibly precious to him. It only made her cry more.

"I don't deserve you. I don't deserve you," she said over and over.

"Jesus, Ally." There was a ragged break in his voice. "Stop saying that. It's not true, and it's killing me."

She shook her head.

"You don't believe me? You don't believe you have a right to be happy?"

"This isn't about happiness. This is about knowing yourself. I should never have let this happen between us. Not when I knew this would happen."

"What is *this,* Ally? Explain it to me."

"You know what it is. I told you. I have to go. I can't stay here. If I try to settle, it'll only be worse in the long run. Harder. Messier."

"Why can't you settle?"

She pushed away from his chest. "Because that's what I do. I leave. I'm my mother's daughter. A faithless, feckless gypsy who can't stick."

"You're the least faithless person I know. As for being a gypsy, I've never met a person who wanted a home more in my life."

Ally stared at him. He lifted a hand and started counting off points.

"Your favorite pastime is reading decorator magazines, looking at other people's homes."

"I like the pictures."

"No, Ally. You like the *homes*. You're a Peeping Tom, a voyeur, looking through the window at what you want."

"That's not true."

"Then there's Dear Gertrude. You think it's an accident that you get so much out of helping other people? That you feel 'connected' to them and like the fact that you help them? You need them every bit as much as they need you, Ally. They're the family you've never allowed yourself to have."

It was like a slap. She flinched.

"*Allowed* myself to have? As though I had a choice, when my mother didn't want me and my grandmother died on me and my aunt resented me. As though I *chose* any of those things."

Tyler didn't say a word. It took a second for her own words to sink in. She pushed herself farther away from him.

"No. This has nothing to do with my family."

"This has everything to do with your family, Ally. This has everything to do with a little kid who learned early on never to get comfortable and never to trust anyone. A lesson you learned so well you've spent your entire adult life rejecting people before they could reject you."

She stood. "You don't know what you're talking about."

Tyler remained on his knees, looking up at her. "I'm not going anywhere, Ally. I love you, and that's never going to change. I'll take any vow, sign any contract, climb any mountain it takes to prove it to you. I love you, and I will never let you down, and I will never stop loving you."

"This isn't about love. I know you love me. It's not about that."

"What's it about, then?"

"I told you. I'm my mother's daughter."

"No, you're not. You're not a selfish, self-involved woman who takes what she wants and then moves on. You're the kind of woman who appoints herself champion for an old man facing his own mortality. You're the kind of woman who doesn't think twice about helping others. You're the kind of woman who cares and loves deeply. And I am not letting you go without a fight, Ally Bishop. I believe in us and I believe in you and I know this is right."

Ally stared at him, utterly caught by his words. Wanting to believe him, so badly.

She closed her eyes and scrubbed her face with her hands. "You don't know what you're talking about."

"I do. I know you. But I don't think you do."

"I have to go."

She left the room blindly, coming to a halt in

the hallway. She looked left, then right, then faced Tyler.

"I need my car keys."

He looked at her for a long moment. "They're on the hook near the phone in the kitchen."

She swiveled and walked to the kitchen. Her keys were hanging next to Tyler's. She grabbed them, then headed for the door.

She half expected Tyler to say something, to try to stop her again, but he didn't. She saw him out of the corner of her eye as she walked past the bedroom, sitting on the bed, looking at his hands.

She made herself keep walking, telling herself that she'd done the hard part. She simply had to leave now, and Tyler could get on with his life without her.

The door swung shut behind her and she stepped out onto the veranda.

He'd be better off without her. He'd see that soon. Once he'd stop being angry with her, he'd see that she'd done the right thing, pulling out before they became so entwined in each others lives that it would be impossible to separate him from her. It was far better that she leave now rather than later, when he would have invested so much more in her.

She carefully didn't think about *her* feelings, about what she would be losing and all that she'd invested in him. The important thing right now was to escape. To remove herself from the temptation that Tyler and his beautiful home and the future he offered represented.

She strode to her car, pressing the remote to unlock it.

I've never met a person who wanted a home more in my life.

She paused, shaken all over again as his words echoed in her mind. No. She slid into the driver's seat. Tyler didn't understand. He was simply seeing things he wanted to see. Trying to hold on to something that was never meant to be.

You're a Peeping Tom, a voyeur, looking through the window at what you want.

She started the car and pulled away from the curb. She liked the pretty pictures in those magazines. That was all. She liked imagining the families who lived in those glossily depicted homes and the parties they had in their perfect yards and the meals they'd cook in their state-of-the-art kitchens—

Her foot eased on the accelerator as it hit her that what she'd just described to herself was, indeed, a form of voyeurism.

So perhaps Tyler had been right about that one thing. But was it so crazy that a woman with no fixed address might fantasize about how the other half lived?

The moment she acknowledged the doubt in her own mind, the rest of Tyler's words rushed her.

This has everything to do with a little kid who learned early on never to get comfortable and never to trust anyone. A lesson you learned so well you've spent your entire adult life rejecting people before they can reject you.

She was shaking so badly she had to stop the car. She felt sick, as though she might throw up. She told herself over and over that Tyler didn't know her, that he didn't know her personal history. But his words struck a deep, resonate chord inside her, a true note on the tuning fork of her emotions.

Things had been good with Daniel before she'd ruined them by chipping away at their happiness and finally leaving. She'd told herself that it was because she was a gypsy, her mother's daughter, that being unable to settle was in her blood. But what if Tyler was right? What if she'd simply hit the emergency button and abandoned the relationship because she'd been afraid that Daniel would abandon her first? What if she'd bailed because she was afraid to trust another person with her happiness?

She wrapped her arms around her torso, her head bowed as she tried to understand herself. She remembered that day by the river and the story she'd told Tyler about her nightmares. She hadn't told him that they'd been worse when her mother had brought her home, that for the first six months she'd lived with her aunt she'd woken with night sweats on a weekly, if not daily, basis. She used to lie in bed trembling in the aftermath, then she used to climb out and creep into her aunt's room to make sure she was still there, that she hadn't been abandoned again. Then, because it was the only way she could calm herself, she would drag her pillow and quilt to her aunt's doorway and sleep across the threshold for the remainder of the night. She'd told herself it was because she wanted the comfort of being close to her aunt, but in a belated flash of insight Ally saw it for what it really was— her childish attempt to prevent her aunt from going anywhere without taking her.

The way her mother had. And her grandmother before her.

Ally pressed her hands to her face, but it didn't stop the tears. All these years she'd been roaming, telling herself it was in her blood—and all the time she'd been running from her childhood fear of being abandoned.

It made her feel small and weak and utterly defenseless. What woman got to the ripe old age of thirty-three before she learned these things about herself?

The kind of person who learned early that pretending fear didn't exist was the only way to survive. The kind of person who was taught through bitter experience that people were unreliable and that love means nothing.

The answer came from the pit of her belly. Visceral. Instinctive. She'd learned early that insecurities and neediness and dependence would not be tolerated. And she'd trained herself to move on whenever she'd felt herself putting down roots and connecting deeply with someone. Neediness equaled rejection.

And the only way to avoid becoming dependent on someone was to leave.

Tyler had been right. About everything. He'd seen the truth of her before she had.

And he still loved her.

The knowledge made her gasp. The ache in her chest expanded.

Tyler loved her. He'd said it a million different ways, with his hands and his eyes and his body and his mouth. He knew her, and he loved her, and he understood her—better, perhaps, than she understood herself.

He said all that—but he didn't try to stop me from leaving. He said he'd fight for me, that he wouldn't give me up—but he let me go.

The voice in her head spoke with a child's fear, trembled with a child's uncertainty.

Then Ally remembered the almost last thing Tyler had said. *I believe in us. I believe in you.*

She reached for the gearshift. Didn't think. Didn't second-guess herself. She put the car in gear and pulled into the street. She'd turned one corner since leaving Tyler's house, so she simply drove in a circle until she'd completed the block and once again turned onto Tyler's street.

She saw his house, lit up with warm golden light. And she saw him, sitting on the bench out the front of his house.

Waiting.

He looked up when he heard her car. Pushed

himself to his feet. She stopped and got out. She walked across the sidewalk and up the path, her heart banging a nervous tattoo against her ribs, her stomach cramping with uncertainty.

What she was about to do was utterly new to her. Revolutionary. She was about to trust another human being. Completely. She was about to hand over her happiness and her safety and her love to another person and trust that he would never grow tired of her or resent her or stop loving her.

She stopped at the bottom of the single step to the veranda. Tyler looked at her, and she could see the pain and doubt in his eyes. But she could also see the hope. The belief.

For a moment the old fear choked her. She closed her eyes for a long second, then opened them again. "I don't know how to do this."

It was true. All her experience was with leaving and running. She didn't know how to stay.

"It's easy. As easy as falling off a tire swing into the river," Tyler said.

He stepped forward and she was in his arms, being held tightly, fiercely, possessively.

"I've got you," he said, and she remembered the other time he'd said those words to her, when he'd stepped between her and a tree.

This man—this amazing man—had protected her with his body. He'd stood by his abusive father with compassion and love until the end, despite great provocation, despite never hearing the words he needed to hear to lay his own ghosts to rest. He'd let her go and waited for her to return. He was all heart.

And he was hers.

If she wanted him. If she had the courage to want him.

"I love you," she said.

"I know. I love you, too, Ally. And I'm not going anywhere."

"Neither am I."

Tyler stilled. Then he pulled back a few inches so he could look into her face. "I'm going to hold you to that."

"Good."

She held his gaze, wanting him to know he could trust her, too. That they were in this thing together.

"I'm sorry for freaking out. So sorry. You must have been—"

He lowered his head and kissed her, cutting off the rest of her words. She kissed him back, meeting his passion with her own. After a few minutes Tyler kissed his way to her ear.

"Let's try this again," he said.

He stepped backward and took her hand, then he led her inside his home. This time, he took her straight to the bedroom.

They moved onto the bed together, needing the confirmation and reassurance of skin on skin. They made love slowly, murmuring praise and encouragement to each other, savoring the closeness. Ally didn't look away from his eyes as she came, baring herself to him utterly. Then she watched as he lost himself, and afterward she curled against him on the bed and listened to the steady, reassuring thump of his heartbeat beneath her ear.

She lifted her head after a few minutes as a thought occurred.

"You were waiting for me out front, weren't you?"

"Of course."

"But what if I hadn't come back?"

"I knew you would. I know you."

She stared at him, stunned by his utter confidence in her. He smiled and reached out to brush her hair from her forehead.

"You once told me that I was the strongest person you knew. Well, you're the strongest person I know, Ally Bishop. You're honest and you're brave and I knew that you'd choose to face your fears rather than run from them."

"I don't deserve you."

"Yes, you do. We deserve each other. If the past few months have taught me anything, it's taught me that. We deserve to be happy, Ally. And we're going to be."

There was so much love and certainty in his face. She touched his cheek, then pressed a kiss to his mouth. Then she settled her head on his chest, over his heart.

"Okay," she said.

"That's it? *Okay?*"

"I trust you."

And she did. With her happiness. With her heart. With her future.

EPILOGUE

One year later

"JUST A LITTLE FARTHER to the left. No, too far. Back a little more to the right. Yes! That's it, perfect," Ally said.

Her husband released his grip on their bulky three-seater sofa and stood, rubbing his back, while his brother did the same at the other end of the sofa.

"You're sure now? You don't want to try it on the other wall?" Tyler asked. "Again."

Ally bit her lip guiltily. "You're sick of me moving the furniture around, aren't you?"

She'd reorganized the house four times in the past twelve months. Couldn't help herself. After years of having no home, she was like a child with a doll-house, determined to explore and enjoy and savor the experience to the full.

Tyler dusted his hands on the seat of his jeans before crossing the room to her side. They'd been married a little more than six months, but the sight of him walking toward her still made her mouth dry. She was beginning to suspect it always would.

He kissed her, then he caught her earlobe between

his thumb and forefinger and caressed it fondly as he smiled into her face.

"Babe, you can mess with the furniture all you like. Whatever tickles your fancy. But we do have guests arriving in about twenty minutes, and I figured you might want to change before they get here."

Ally looked down at herself. She'd been in the yard, planting out the annuals she'd bought to give the garden a bit of extra color for their delayed Christmas party for Tyler's staff. The workshop had been so overwhelmed with orders prior to the festive season that they'd opted to do a late celebration after Christmas when everyone was more able to enjoy it.

"You really think your staff are going to notice if I'm wearing gumboots and have a little mud on my shorts?" she asked.

"They'll be crushed. You know they have a very high opinion of Gertrude." He patted her on the backside. "Why don't you slip into the shower and I'll join you in a minute?"

There was a light in his eyes that Ally recognized only too well. She smiled, her gaze dropping to the swathe of tanned skin visible at his neckline.

Jon made a disbelieving noise in the background. "Seriously, guys. The honeymoon was over months ago."

Tyler didn't bother turning around as he ushered Ally toward the hallway.

"Shut up. Make yourself useful and warm up the barbecue."

"Sure. But what should I tell everyone when they get here and you two are missing?" Jon said.

"We won't be missing," Ally said.

Tyler gave her a knowing look. Her heart gave an excited little leap.

"Improvise," he said over his shoulder.

Then he hustled Ally into the en suite bathroom before she could say anything else.

"We can't be late for our own party," she said as Tyler slid his hands beneath her grubby T-shirt.

"Have I ever mentioned how much I love a woman in gumboots?" he said as he walked her backward until she was pressed against the tiled wall.

"No."

"Well, I do. Especially when that woman is you."

He kissed her and the protest she'd been about to voice died in her throat.

"You really don't mind that I keep rearranging the house?" she said as he pushed her top up and started working on the clasp for her bra.

"I'd say if I did," he said, his hungry gaze roaming over her breasts.

"I'm pretty sure I'll grow out of it."

Tyler caught her chin so she had to look into his eyes. "I don't care, Ally."

She relaxed. "Good."

"You know what would be even better? If you weren't wearing these shorts," Tyler said, frowning at the bulky knot in the drawstring at her waist.

"Huh. How did that happen?"

They bent their heads together as they tried to unravel the knot. After a few seconds, the absurdity of the situation hit Ally. She glanced up into her husband's face and found a smile curling the corners of his mouth.

Their shared sense of humor was one of many joys in their relationship. Over the past twelve months, she'd discovered so many things about both herself and the man she'd married. She'd learned that trust was possible, that fears were bearable and that love was not a static thing. Instead, it deepened and broadened and grew richer with every day.

"Scissors?" she suggested.

"Definitely."

He pulled away to go find them, but she caught his shoulder.

"I love you, Tyler Adamson."

"I love you, too, Mrs. Adamson."

She let him go and settled against the wall to wait.

He wouldn't be gone long.

And she wasn't going anywhere.

* * * * *

COMING NEXT MONTH

Available March 8, 2011

REQUEST YOUR FREE BOOKS!

2 FREE NOVELS PLUS 2 FREE GIFTS!

Silhouette®

ROMANTIC SUSPENSE

Sparked by Danger, Fueled by Passion.

YES! Please send me 2 FREE Silhouette® Romantic Suspense novels and my 2 FREE gifts (gifts are worth about $10). After receiving them, if I don't wish to receive any more books, I can return the shipping statement marked "cancel." If I don't cancel, I will receive 4 brand-new novels every month and be billed just $4.24 per book in the U.S. or 4.99 per book in Canada. That's a saving of at least 15% off the cover price! It's quite a bargain! Shipping and handling is just 50¢ per book in the U.S. and 75¢ per book in Canada.* I understand that accepting the 2 free books and gifts places me under no obligation to buy anything. I can always return a shipment and cancel at any time. Even if I never buy another book, the two free books and gifts are mine to keep forever.

240/340 SDN FC95

Name	(PLEASE PRINT)

Address	Apt. #

City	State/Prov.	Zip/Postal Code

Signature (if under 18, a parent or guardian must sign)

Mail to the Reader Service:
IN U.S.A.: P.O. Box 1867, Buffalo, NY 14240-1867
IN CANADA: P.O. Box 609, Fort Erie, Ontario L2A 5X3

Not valid for current subscribers to Silhouette Romantic Suspense books.

Want to try two free books from another line?
Call 1-800-873-8635 or visit www.ReaderService.com.

Terms and prices subject to change without notice. Prices do not include applicable taxes. Sales tax applicable in N.Y. Canadian residents will be charged applicable taxes. Offer not valid in Quebec. This offer is limited to one order per household. All orders subject to credit approval. Credit or debit balances in a customer's account(s) may be offset by any other outstanding balance owed by or to the customer. Please allow 4 to 6 weeks for delivery. Offer available while quantities last.

Your Privacy—The Reader Service is committed to protecting your privacy. Our Privacy Policy is available online at www.ReaderService.com or upon request from the Reader Service.

We make a portion of our mailing list available to reputable third parties that offer products we believe may interest you. If you prefer that we not exchange your name with third parties, or if you wish to clarify or modify your communication preferences, please visit us at www.ReaderService.com/consumerschoice or write to us at Reader Service Preference Service, P.O. Box 9062, Buffalo, NY 14269. Include your complete name and address.

SRSI1

USA TODAY *bestselling author Lynne Graham*
is back with a thrilling new trilogy
SECRETLY PREGNANT, CONVENIENTLY WED

Three heroines must marry alpha males to keep
their dreams…but Alejandro, Angelo and Cesario
are not about to be tamed!

Book 1—JEMIMA'S SECRET
Available March 2011 from Harlequin Presents®.

JEMIMA yanked open a drawer in the sideboard to fi
Alfie's birth certificate. Her son was her husband's chi
It was a question of telling the truth whether she liked it
not. She extended the certificate to Alejandro.

"This has to be nonsense," Alejandro asserted.

"Well, if you can find some other way of explaining h
I managed to give birth by that date and Alfie not be you
I'd like to hear it," Jemima challenged.

Alejandro glanced up, golden eyes bright as blades a
as dangerous. "All this proves is that you must still ha
been pregnant when you walked out on our marriage
does not automatically follow that the child is mine."

"'I know it doesn't suit you to hear this news now an
really didn't want to tell you. But I can't lie to you about
Someday Alfie may want to look you up and get acquainte

"If what you have just told me is the truth, if that li
boy does prove to be mine, it was vindictive and extrem
selfish of you to leave me in ignorance!"

Jemima paled. "When I left you, I had no idea that I w
still pregnant."

"Two years is a long period of time, yet you made
attempt to inform me that I might be a father. I will w
DNA tests to confirm your claim before I make any de

ion about what I want to do."

"Do as you like," she told him curtly. "*I* know who Alfie's father is and there has never been any doubt of his identity."

"I will make arrangements for the tests to be carried out and I will see you again when the result is available," Alejandro drawled with lashings of dark Spanish masculine reserve.

"I'll contact a solicitor and start the divorce," Jemima proffered in turn.

Alejandro's eyes narrowed in a piercing scrutiny that made her uncomfortable. "It would be foolish to do anything before we have that DNA result."

"I disagree," Jemima flashed back. "I should have applied for a divorce the minute I left you!"

Alejandro quirked an ebony brow. "And why didn't you?"

Jemima dealt him a fulminating glance but said nothing, merely moving past him to open her front door in a blunt invitation for him to leave.

"I'll be in touch," he delivered on the doorstep.

What is Alejandro's next move? Perhaps rekindling their marriage is the only solution! But will Jemima agree?

Find out in Lynne Graham's
exciting new romance
JEMIMA'S SECRET

Available March 2011
from Harlequin Presents®.

Start your Best Body today with these top 3 nutrition tips!

1. SHOP THE PERIMETER OF THE GROCERY STORE: The good stuff—fruits, veggies, lean proteins and dairy—always line the outer edges of the store. When you veer into the center aisles, you enter the temptation zone, where the unhealthy foods live.

2. WATCH PORTION SIZES: Most portion sizes in restaurants are nearly twice the size of a true serving and at home, it's easy to "clean your plate." Use these easy serving guidelines:
- Protein: the palm of your hand
- Grains or Fruit: a cup of your hand
- Veggies: the palm of two open hands

3. USE THE RAINBOW RULE FOR PRODUCE: Your produce drawers should be filled with every color of fruits and vegetables. The greater the variety, the more vitamins and other nutrients you add to your diet.

Find these and many more helpful tips in

YOUR BEST BODY NOW

by

TOSCA RENO

WITH STACY BAKER

Bestselling Author of
THE EAT-CLEAN DIET®

Available wherever books are sold!